OWNER OF A LONELY HEART

KIRSTEN S. BLACKETER

DEDICATION

Cauliflower.

TABLE OF CONTENTS

CHAPTER ONE
CLAUDE

Hell's Kitchen NYC, December 1985

I've had my fill of violence. I've had more than my fill of conflict and death, more than most people know. It's left a sour taste in my mouth. As a veteran of an unpopular war, I bear a daily reminder of the impact violence has had on my life, but I've learned to cope with it. Now I'm a pacifist, and I own a bar in Hell's Kitchen. That suits me right down to the ground. I tried joining the police force when I came home, but I didn't make the cut. I guess having lost my hand and the lower part of my arm put me at a disadvantage. Sacrifice always puts you at a disadvantage.

My brother is a homicide detective. A few months ago, he nearly died in the line of duty, which finally pushed me over the edge. I have no intention of putting myself in the midst of a horde of assholes with guns and itchy trigger fingers ever again. My life might not be perfect, but I've worked hard for it. I'm not about to throw it away playing the hero.

The door swings open on a gust of December wind, complete with copious amounts of snow. Such a storm is uncommon this early in the year, but it happens. The new arrival manages to close the door, then whips off the scarf around his head.

"Hey, Tom." I reach for the vodka. He's a regular who orders the same drink every night—a double shot of Russia's finest in a chilled glass.

"Claude." He sidles up to the bar, brushing off the remnants of the storm outside. "Looks like the weathermen were wrong…again."

I feel a lopsided smile on my lips as I set the glass in front of him. "You sure you don't want coffee? I can add some whiskey to spice it up."

Tom crinkles his nose at the mention of the drink. Even though many of my patrons come from hardy Irish stock, there are a few who don't have an ounce of Celtic heritage in their blood. Tom's family came from Russia, and he served in the Navy during the Korean War. After my honorable discharge from the Army, I took over my grandfather's pub, and when Tom stumbled in, our military bond made us fast friends despite a twenty-year age gap.

He taps the glass on the bar and lifts it in salute before downing the contents. Then he tells me about his day.

I soak it in.

This is my life. Service before self. Simple. Unfettered.

Lonely.

I have my faithful patrons and my family, but there's an uneasy distance between life and me. Since the war, I've played it safe, venturing only far enough to ensure the bar is taken care of and my brother stays out of trouble.

But he's not my responsibility anymore. He's got Quinn. She's good for him. They're a match made in chaos. That doesn't surprise me. Grant has always been a magnet for trouble, and Quinn personifies it.

I listen absently as Tom tells me about his adventure to the fish market across town. It's the same every week, but I don't mind indulging an old man his stories. It goes hand in hand with being a bartender. I watch, listen, and serve those who need a drink, an ear, or a smile.

A few more people arrive, coats and heads covered in white. Guess the storm must have picked up. They take a corner booth, and Sam scurries over to take their order.

He brings me the drink order before retreating to the small kitchen. We serve simple fare, burgers and fries, soups—hearty bar food to soak up the alcohol. No one comes here for the food.

The Black Penny is nothing fancy, but she's mine. My grandfather opened the bar before World War II. When dad didn't want to take over, Pap turned to me. I was a broken kid, fresh home from war. I didn't know the first thing about running a business, but he took me under his wing and showed me the ropes. Even without a left hand, I managed to pick it up quickly. Gave me hope I could make something of myself.

When Pap passed, he left me not only the bar but the building. I don't know where I'd be without him. His final request was twofold. Keep the bar in the family. Find a girl to make that happen.

It's been ten years, and I haven't been able to fulfill that promise. No one wants a warworn, one-armed bartender.

I can't say I blame them.

Tom waves me over for a refill. "Hell of a storm out there. Don't usually see these sorts until January."

"That's true." I pour him another round.

The door bursts open. A dark figure stumbles in, snow curling in a tornado around them as they struggle to close the door. Once they succeed, they collapse against it.

A brick drops into my stomach when the new arrival turns toward me.

Wide blue eyes the color of summer skies peer out from beneath long, thick, dark hair tangled with snowflakes. An oversized winter coat encases her whole body, gaping just enough so the sequined fabric beneath could catch the light. She moves like a skittish cat, shying away from light, from people. Then she sees me, and relief fills her delicate features. She rushes to the bar. Tearstained streaks of mascara stream down her cheeks. She leans her trembling hands on the counter, and her gaze darts around the room, searching for an oncoming threat.

"Can I help you, ma'am?" I lean close and keep my voice low in an attempt to soothe her. I'm afraid one quick movement or loud noise will shatter her fragile composure.

Flecks of white cling to her lashes. They flutter as she looks up at me, her eyes bloodshot and rimmed with tear-smudged mascara. "Do…do you have a restroom?" Her voice is low, and I hear a tremor beneath the words.

Her expensive-looking wool coat is open at her throat,

exposing the delicate curve of her neck and a fancy gown beneath. My gaze lingers on the white glittering fabric…stained red. *Blood.*

"Yes, in the back." I point to the back of the bar. "Are you okay?" I keep my tone low and steady, but concern laces every word. "Are you bleeding?"

"I'm fine." She clutches the lapels of her coat, pulling the garment closed. "If someone comes looking for me, I'm not here, okay?"

I nod, but before I can press further, she darts to the back of the bar and disappears down the hallway.

I should check on her, make sure she's okay.

Tom pipes up from his nearby perch. "Poor kid looks like she's running from something."

"Yeah." I rub my hand across my jaw and look toward the back of the bar. Judging from her clothes and demeanor, she's not from around here. Probably an uptown girl caught in the wrong neighborhood. High-maintenance, with money burning a hole in her purse. A high-class broad looking for a good time. Not typical for this part of town. Strange.

As I wipe down the bar, the door flies open with another burst of cold air, swirling more snow into the room. Three men step through. The last one closes the door and stands against it, a guard blocking any possible escape. All three reek of power and corruption. Mafia.

The leader steps forward, his face half-covered with a bloodstained rag pressed to his nose. He pulls the cloth away and scans the bar with a sharp eye. The bridge of his nose is crooked, his fair skin bruised and smeared red. A trickle of blood runs down his lips. He wipes it away in irritation.

Perhaps it wasn't her blood after all.

Her plea echoes in my mind. *I'm not here.*

Tom and I exchange a look before he returns his attention to the empty glass before him.

"Can I get you gentlemen a drink?" I lean against the bar to hide the nervous energy pulsing at the base of my skull, warning me nothing good can come from this. From *them.*

The battered leader steps up to the bar. Bloodstained and proud, he looks like a warrior from a bygone era, vengeance in his blue eyes. He wears an expensive, well-tailored suit, but red mars the white dress shirt. He presses the bloody handkerchief back to his bruised nose.

"Did a woman just come in here?" His gaze fixes on me.

"Nope." I lift one shoulder, a halfhearted shrug, as I wipe down the counter.

The man's eyes narrow as if searching me for the truth. "You're sure?"

"Positive." I gesture to the nearly empty bar. "Can I get you a drink?"

A sneer curls the rich asshole's lip. He shoves away from the bar with a growl and motions to his men. "Look around."

Without delay, the two men split up and quickly search the bar. They disappear toward the bathroom.

My heart ices over. There's no way to warn her, to hide her. I maintain my calm and busy myself with small tasks behind the bar.

The bloody bastard swears, wiping more blood from his upper lip. His men reappear and shake their heads.

"She's not here."

"Fuck." Irritation radiates from the single word. "Let's go. The bitch can find her own way home. I'll deal with her then."

Without another word, the three men exit the bar, leaving a chill in their wake. I clench the rag in my fist and command my heart to stop racing.

"You think she went out the back?" Tom asks, his question quiet.

"I don't know." Tossing the towel aside, I head for the back of the bar.

When I pass Sam, I give him whispered instructions to watch for customers and yell if there's trouble.

With a look of confusion, he nods before joining Tom. He'll fill him in on the details.

Right now, I need answers, and the only way I'll get them is if I find the beautiful, bloodstained debutante hiding somewhere in my building.

Chapter Two
Gwen

He's going to kill me.

Standing in the small, two-stall bathroom, I stare at the wreck reflected in the mirror. My hair's a knotted mess, my makeup smeared beyond redemption. I groan when I pull open my wool coat to reveal the bloody bodice of the ivory Gucci gown I got for my birthday last year.

When I jammed my purse in his face, I was prepared for his rage but not for the blood. The struggle ruined my gown. How I managed to get out of the car and away from Nick, I'll never know. I suppose a few well-placed kicks must have given me the opening I needed. Thank God for the snowstorm. It covered me long enough to find this bar to hide.

I use a wet towel to clean my face, but the dress is unsalvageable.

Two gruff voices echo in the hallway beyond the door. I grab the towel and hide in a stall, locking it behind me. Carefully, I climb onto the toilet, cradling my gown so it won't show beneath the partitions.

Someone kicks open the door.

I clap my hand over my mouth to silence shaky breaths. Whoever it is, I shrink at their presence.

"She in there?" a deep, familiar voice asks.

"Nothing."

"Let's check the rest of the joint."

Footsteps recede, and the door closes softly behind them. I lean my head against the wall and breathe deeply. Focusing on a faint water stain on the ceiling panel, I count to one hundred. When I'm sure they're gone, I step down and sit on the toilet seat.

After a few more minutes, my racing heart slows to a steady rhythm. I dab the towel against my neck to wipe away the sweat and blood.

What the hell am I going to do now?

I can't go back to Nick. Not after that…not after he asked me to…

I pinch my eyes closed.

No. I won't do it.

There's no way I can crawl back to my parents either. Not after what happened. My father will force me to do whatever Nick wants. They want to keep him happy. He's my fiancé after all. Nothing, aside from death, can change that.

I hang my head and let the tears flow. This isn't what I want. I know what people see when I walk into the room. A spoiled rich girl with more beauty than brains. A shiny treasure to wear on special occasions.

Fuck that. Fuck them.

I'm more than that, and if I need to burn some bridges to secure my independence, then I will.

A soft knock at the door disturbs my solitude. I hold my breath.

"They're gone." The bartender's gentle tone drifts into the empty room. "Can I come in?"

I slowly stand and unlock the stall door. When I step out, I'm struck by the sight of the tall bartender, the bathroom door cracked enough for him to speak quietly to me. His long hair and neatly trimmed goatee hide a pair of kind brown eyes and a tender smile.

"Thank you." I smooth my hands over my coat. "I'm sorry to put you in such an awkward situation."

He meets my gaze. "You needed help."

I nod and turn away. "I don't want to cause any trouble. I should go."

The bartender refuses to let me pass. "Not tonight. Not in that storm." He pushes the door open and steps back. "Follow me."

We walk down the hallway until we reach a door labeled

Office. The light flickers overhead. He reaches up to tap the fixture. The light resumes its full brilliance and holds firm.

I study his broad shoulders as he opens the door and switches on a lamp beside the desk.

"Come in." He rounds the desk and pulls open a few drawers, searching for something. When he stands, he holds out a stack of clothing with one hand. "You might want to change."

I take the garments with a grateful smile. "Thank you."

"Can't have you walking around looking like you just walked away from a murder scene." He smiles, and my heart softens at his thoughtfulness. "You can change in here. Just leave your clothes on the floor by the desk. Come out to the bar when you're ready."

Stepping aside, I allow him space to pass me. His scent surrounds me, pine and Old Spice with a darker note beneath it. Something only belonging to him, if I had to guess. It's comforting, like a glass of mulled wine on Christmas Eve.

He pauses in the doorway and glances at me.

"You sure you're okay? Not bleeding or injured?"

"I'm fine. I promise."

"Okay." He pulls the door closed behind him, leaving me alone in the office.

I wiggle out of the oversized coat and struggle to find the zipper on my dress. After a few minutes, I manage to unstick the zipper, and I peel the damp Gucci gown from my skin. Wadding it in a ball, I set it on the floor behind the desk. Gooseflesh pricks my skin, and I quickly pull on the oversized sweatshirt and sweatpants.

They hang loose in places, but it's a relief to not be wearing something tight and gaudy for once. I've caught plenty of grief from my mother for my ample curves. As if I had a choice. I wasn't blessed with a small waist or petite breasts. All of my garments are altered to fit, much to my mother's irritation.

Knowing I don't have anyone to impress or an image to project provides a keen sense of relief I haven't felt in a long time. I rake my fingers through my hair and twist it over my shoulder. I ensure my purse is still tucked safely inside my coat before draping it over the chair behind the desk. There's not much in it, just my pills, a compact, lipstick, and a few dollars. Still, I don't want to forget it. With a deep breath, I gather what strength remains and slip out of the office, leaving my coat and purse behind.

When I reach the bar, it's empty except for the bartender and a waiter wiping down the tables. The bartender's stern expression softens to a kind smile when he sees me, and he gestures to an empty chair at the bar.

"Would you like something to eat?" he asks as he works, placing the glasses on a shelf behind the register. He watches me in the mirror's reflection.

I shake my head.

"Drink?"

"After the night I've had…yeah, I could use a drink." I scan the bottles, searching for a selection. "I'll have—"

"Let me guess."

Stunned, I watch him retrieve a glass before turning for a bottle. With one hand, he scoops ice and pours it into the shaker. Every move is done with his right hand. That's when I realize my knight in shining armor is missing his left hand. I mean, I noticed something was different, but my addled brain didn't register what wasn't there.

He moves with grace, perfectly pouring the liquor, adding ingredients with ease. When he lifts the shaker in one massive palm, I'm convinced it's magic. He lifts the top, strains the concoction over ice, and adds a sprig of rosemary and a long thin strip of cucumber before topping it with a lime wedge.

"Try this." He sets the drink on a napkin and slides it toward me.

"What is it?" I raise the glass and inhale. The rosemary and lime mix with the herbal bite of the liquor. It smells divine.

"I call it a Tipsy Rose."

I snort. "Someone's been watching *The Golden Girls*."

"What's *The Golden Girls*?" He cocks his head.

I can tell his look of confusion is genuine.

"It's a television show." I wave my hand. "Never mind."

I take a sip, and the flavor surrounds me like a warm hug. It's a complex mix of sweet and floral with a bite of citrus. I feel like I've stepped into a fairy-tale forest, indulged in a heavenly drink created by elves. "Oh my God. That's amazing."

"I thought you'd like it." He grins, and I'm pretty sure he's pleased with himself.

"You're good." I take another drink, savoring the flavor. "How did you get so good at mixing drinks?"

"Practice."

"That explains a lot." I cradle the glass in my hands. "So do you have a name?"

"Claude." He brushes his hair away from his face. "Owner and proprietor of the Black Penny."

"Claude? That's a very French name for the owner of an Irish pub."

He shrugs. "My mother was obsessed with Monet."

His response stuns me. I'm not sure what to say without sounding overly inquisitive, but the desire to know more tugs at the back of my mind. I sip my drink to fill the lapse in conversation.

"And what about you?"

My face warms under the intensity of his gaze. "Gigi."

"Looks like my parents weren't the only ones obsessed with France." Claude chuckles.

"It's a nickname. My friends call me Gigi, but my name is Gwen." I curse the comfort of his presence for making me give my real name rather than an alias. It's too late. I can't take it back. I can only hope he doesn't read tabloids or watch the news. Once my family realizes I'm missing, there will be a citywide search. I'd rather blend into the woodwork and disappear than go back to my gilded prison.

"It's a lovely name." He smiles, and my heart softens again. "Are we friends now, Gwen?"

"You saved me, so I would say that makes us a bit more than friends." I lift my glass in salute. "To unexpected friendships."

Claude lifts a glass of water and meets my toast.

"It's bad luck to toast with water," I tease.

"I don't drink." He sets the glass aside.

"A bartender who doesn't indulge in alcohol? How odd." I chuckle. Am I tipsy already? Lord, what is in this drink?

"You'd be surprised." His cryptic answer lingers in the air. "The storm's getting bad. I'm going to close up. Make yourself comfortable." With a small salute, he goes through a small, swinging door.

I am surprised. I chew my lip and slowly finish my drink. This night has certainly taken a strange but welcome turn. My desperate escape from Nick led me to this place, and I couldn't be more thankful for the kindness of this one-armed bartender. He went above and beyond to make sure I was safe.

I don't think I've ever had anyone do anything for me purely out of the goodness of their heart. Normally, I'm surrounded by people who are willing to do things for me, but they always want something in return. Nothing is selfless when people know my name. My family. Everyone is a vulture, searching for the next score.

I've worked hard over the past ten years to put as much distance as possible between myself and those who would use me for their own gain. And yet, my father arranged my marriage to Nicholas DeLuca, the son of one of the most prominent mob bosses in New York City. I can't fight it. I'm bound by blood. At some point, they'll find me. They'll come for me. I'll go, kicking and screaming, biting and clawing. I will never give Nick the satisfaction of thinking he's tamed me. I'd rather throw myself off the Brooklyn Bridge.

If I could have my way, I'd disappear, vanish into the wind, start over. But how can I do that? I have no money, no prospects, no skills. I've never lived on my own or had a job. It's not that I can't take care of myself or do work. It's that they won't let me. What I want doesn't matter. I'm just a pawn in their endless game of chess. They'll sacrifice me without hesitation.

Claude appears from the hallway with a mop and a bucket. He crosses the room and turns off the sign before locking the door. He flicks a set of switches, dimming the lights until only the back of the bar remains illuminated

The waiter appears and takes the mop from Claude's hand.

"Do you have somewhere to go where you'll be safe?" Claude takes two tentative steps in my direction.

My mouth goes dry. With those broad shoulders and sharp features, he's like a towering oak tree reaching for the sky. Handsome in a strange, offhand way. His heavy brows and full lips contrast the bold angles of his face. A tiny, faded scar mars his cheek, surrounded by small, dark freckles. He's the night sky dotted with constellations and mystery. Those fathomless eyes search mine as he waits for a response.

"No. I don't. I'll figure something out." I smile, but it's forced and makes my throat burn.

"You can stay with me if you'd like. I have an apartment upstairs." He clears his throat. "I mean, for the night…until the storm lets up."

He seems flustered at the prospect, and I find it endearing. I don't like the idea of accepting charity, but I don't have much choice. Besides, I'd rather stay with this kind stranger than return to the lion's den and be devoured.

"Thank you, Claude. I appreciate the offer." I stand, bringing us toe to toe. "Are you sure I won't be intruding?"

"Positive." He rocks back on his heels, his throat working. "There's plenty of room."

There's something strangely sweet about this man. I study him carefully, weighing my options. I have no money, no prospects…and it's too late to find somewhere else to crash. Even then, they'll find me.

No, this is the best place. At least I'll be able to breathe freely for a few minutes without my family and Nick stalking my every move.

When my father finds out what I did, he'll force me to marry Nick. I wish he'd cut me off without regret. Somehow, that would be a more comforting solution, considering the alternative. Starting over without a penny to my name would be easier than enduring what Nick has planned for me.

Tonight, though, I have a reprieve. This is my chance to

figure out what I want. How far I'm willing to go to break free from these vultures who would prey on me without thought.

"I'll stay." I smile at Claude, and the motion makes my cheeks ache. This time, it's sincere.

Chapter Three
Claude

Her smile leaves me devastated. There's something soft and vulnerable about her. The hesitant way she speaks counters the confidence in her words. Underneath that ruffled exterior, she's resilient and determined. She's a beacon of light in this dark, lonely bar. I'd be a fool to push her away in her hour of need. My mother raised me better than that.

"Come on, then." I pass her, heading for the stairs.

I don't need to turn to know she's following. Her presence radiates warmth and awareness.

Grant would call me a fool for inviting a perfect stranger into my home, but didn't he do the exact same thing just a few months ago? I mean, it was a little more complicated than that. The woman was a cat burglar turned murder witness who ended up on my doorstep, bloody and damn near unconscious. She dragged in a whole mess of trouble, but it was worth it. Quinn makes my brother happy. And surely, he wouldn't begrudge me the same hope.

Not that I expect anything from my time with this beautiful stranger. She's leaps and bounds out of my league, likely lives in an ivory tower. That bloody dress she was wearing was probably worth more than my whole year's income. And she didn't bat an eyelash at the ruined gown. I doubt she's had to struggle a day in her lavish life.

By the time we reach my apartment on the third floor, I'm exhausted by the argument in my head. It doesn't matter who she is or where she comes from. She needs help, and I can make sure she's safe and warm. It's the honorable thing to do.

Except…the way I want to unravel her secrets is far from honorable. I shake away the nagging desperation and focus on the door. It swings open, and I gesture for her to enter.

She swans into my world, wearing a pair of borrowed sweatpants and an oversized sweatshirt. Damn if she doesn't look like a queen surveying her kingdom, her curious gaze sweeping the room.

"It's so quaint." She brushes a hand over the afghan on the back of the sofa. "And clean."

"You sound surprised." I close the door and lock it behind us.

"I guess I am." Her cheeks flare a delicate shade of rose.

"Most people are." I gesture to the doors on my right. "Shower's through here and the bedroom's here. There's a door inside the bathroom to the bedroom. You'll find some toiletries you can use—shampoo, soap, new toothbrush under the sink."

"You sure you're not a Boy Scout?" She leans against the sofa, watching me.

"I was. Made Eagle at fifteen." I squirm under her scrutiny.

"I guess it left an impression."

Her smile warms me, like a strong shot of whiskey.

"It did." I grab two glasses and get water for each of us. "Can I ask you a question?"

"Depends on the question." She shifts.

So she is hiding from something.

"That guy who came looking for you, did you do that to his face?" I point to my own nose before handing her the glass.

"Yes. But he deserved it."

"I have no doubt he deserved it." I sip my water. "Who was he?"

"My fiancé."

The sharp word echoes through my skull, and an anchor drops in my stomach. "Your *fiancé?*"

"Well, kind of. Sort of." She struggles to find the words, but I'm lost in the fact that she's taken by someone who clearly doesn't deserve her.

What the hell am I thinking? I barely know this woman…and yet, I'm captivated by her. Hopeless.

"It's complicated." She sighs and shakes her head.

"I understand."

Judging by her stance, it's more complicated than she's willing to discuss right now. I drop it. If she wants to tell me, she'll do it when she's ready. After what she's been through, anyone would be terrified. But she's a fighter, if the bloodstains on her dress and her fiancé's broken nose are any indication. Strength flows through her veins.

"Can I ask you a question now?" She blinks at me.

"Anything."

"Are you hiring?"

I choke on my water. "What?"

"In the bar, do you need an extra hand?"

She closes her eyes and curses under her breath at the thoughtless use of the phrase. It doesn't bother me.

"I don't want your pity or charity. I'll work to earn my keep."

"Do you plan on sticking around?" I lean against the counter. "What about your fiancé?"

"Fuck him." Gwen clears her throat. "If you let me stay, I'll work hard. I promise."

My mood improves at her vehement response. Perhaps there's hope after all. "What experience do you have?"

"None."

"Then why should I hire you?"

She bristles and drops her gaze. After a few moments, those blue eyes meet mine, determination in their depths. "Because I need work, and I like it here."

I fold my arms across my chest. "How do you make a Manhattan?"

"Whiskey and vermouth."

A laugh escapes me. "It's more nuanced than that, sweetheart."

Her body tenses. "Then teach me. I'm a fast learner."

"Maybe tomorrow."

"So I'm hired?" A smile erupts across that sinfully plush mouth.

"I never said that." I push away from the counter and head

for the bedroom. I pause in the doorway, then turn. "One more thing."

"Huh?"

Those blue eyes flash in my direction, and I'm momentarily blinded by need pulsing through me.

"What did you do with the dress?"

"Oh." Her cheeks flush again, and she straightens. "It's on the floor behind the desk in your office."

"I'll take care of it." I turn on the lights in the bathroom and bedroom before returning to the living room. "You can take a shower and rest."

"Thank you, Claude." She crosses the room, leaving the sweet scent of honeysuckle in her wake.

"Let me know if you need anything." I head out to give her some space.

Alone on the landing outside the apartment, I lean against the door. What the hell am I thinking? The temptation is too great. It's more than I expected.

This gorgeous—obviously wealthy—woman has secrets. I don't hold it against her, but it puts me in an awkward position. What if her family comes looking for her? What if *he* comes back?

I'll cross that bridge when we get there. Tonight, I just have to make it work. It's only for one night. Tomorrow, I'll help her find a safe place and a job if that's what she wants.

But do I want her to stay with me? To work in my bar?

Yes, my mind insists without hesitation.

I make my way down the stairs and open the office door. Inside, I find the gown, wrapped in a tight ball, tucked behind my desk. I unravel it and savor her sweet scent clinging to the fabric. The stain is embedded deep in the beading, beyond salvation. Unless…

I pick up the phone and call Rob. He answers, even though it's after midnight.

"Hello?"

"Rob, it's Claude from the Black Penny."

"Is everything okay?" The concern is clear in his voice.

"Everything's fine." I study the intricate stitching on the

gown and note the tag. "Had a patron come in tonight with blood on a fancy Gucci gown. Any idea how to get the stain out?"

Rob laughs. "What makes you think I know how to get blood out of a Gucci gown?"

"You work in a hospital. I just figured you'd know some tricks since you probably get blood on your clothes sometimes."

"Peroxide works, but…hold on." The chatter in the background turns into a full-blown argument.

"Hello?" A woman's voice comes through the line. "This is Marcy. Who's this?"

"Ma'am. This is Claude from the Black Penny. I apologize for waking you."

"You didn't wake me." She huffs. "I heard Rob mention Gucci and peroxide in the same breath. Do *not* listen to him."

"Would you happen to know what to use, then? It's her favorite gown, and I'd hate for it to be ruined."

A heavy sigh fills the void. "Send it over. I'll take care of it." She gives me her address.

I balance the phone against my shoulder as I write everything down. "I'll have it delivered tomorrow. Thank you, ma'am."

"You're welcome. Good night."

"Night." I hang up the phone and neatly fold the gown, tucking it into a trash bag. Tomorrow, I'll pay someone to deliver it.

Flicking off the light, I grab her purse and coat before locking the office and returning upstairs. Inside my apartment, the air has shifted. It's warmer, lighter…sweeter. I lean my ear against the bathroom door and hear the shower.

Quietly, I slip into the bedroom to retrieve the sweatpants and tee shirt I sleep in. The soft strains of her voice echo through the gap left by the slightly open bathroom door. It takes all my restraint not to peek in and drink my fill.

Chastising myself, I open the drawer to pull out a soft pair of pajamas. After laying them on the bed, I retreat to the living room. A quick change, and I'm as comfortable as I can be with a naked bombshell in the next room. In my bed.

I fluff a pillow and lay on the couch. I drape the afghan from the back of the couch over me, struggling to cover my feet.

In the next room, she moves and the noise makes me restless. I close my eyes, but all I can picture is her round face, her sea-blue eyes, her dangerous curves covered in sequins and blood.

For years, I've been comfortable with my life. With my status as a bachelor. Even with the promise to my grandfather hanging over my head, I was at peace with the cards I'd been dealt.

But now I can't help but dream of something…someone, who might be more trouble than she's worth. Damn my conscience.

CHAPTER FOUR
GWEN

His absence should relieve me, but it leaves me aching.

I'm in a stranger's apartment, in an uncomfortable and unfamiliar part of town. There's nothing about this situation that should give me comfort…and yet, I'm at ease.

Guilt pricks me for not being honest with him. I should have told Claude the truth. Who I am. Who the asshole downstairs was. I can't bring myself to reveal such details. Not yet. I feel horrible, especially when he so selflessly opened his home to me.

While he's gone, I trace my fingers along the back of the sofa. It's faded with fraying rips and tears, but it's clean. My gaze drifts around the small apartment. A bookcase lines the wall next to the bedroom. The sofa faces a television against the wall, between two windows. The galley kitchen opens to a small dining area with a table and two chairs. The furniture is worn and well-loved, holdovers from the seventies.

It's surprisingly tidy. Every surface dusted, the blanket on the sofa folded. I wander into the bedroom and find the same fastidious organization. A neatly made bed with sharp corners, two nightstands flanking it. One holds a cream-colored lamp and a stack of books, piled five deep. I scan the titles—all of them are Stephen King except one, a worn copy of Shakespeare's comedies.

I chuckle. My savior doesn't look like a horror or Shakespeare fan. He looks…well, he doesn't look like someone who likes to read. I guess that makes me a piss-poor judge of someone based on looks.

He's different from anyone I've ever known. My family. My fiancé. My so-called friends. It's refreshing to meet someone from outside my narrow social circle.

If my father knew, he'd rage, lock me in my room, restrict what little freedom I have. He's made demands on me for years, but this last act of betrayal has left me clawing to get away, desperate and with complete disregard for the consequences.

I can't go back to my father. To that family. Not when Nick is the person I'd really be going back to. I refuse to bind myself to a man who will exploit me for his own selfish gain. To a man who doesn't truly care about what happens to me. He'll use me until I no longer serve a purpose, then he'll discard me.

No. I can't go back. I *refuse.*

Groaning, I sit on the bed and take off my three-inch heels. The carpet soothes the aching soles of my feet when I retreat into the bathroom to turn on the shower.

There's a fresh, folded towel waiting on the counter. I appreciate the cleanliness and order, but I feel like I'm intruding on his personal space.

Quickly, I strip out of the borrowed clothes and push them off to the side before stepping into the spray of warm water. I manage to scrub whatever blood remains with a new bar of Irish Spring soap. My brow furrows at the coconut-scented shampoo and conditioner on the shelf. I use them, and the delicate scent indicates I must not be the only woman who uses Claude's shower.

Does he have a girlfriend? A wife? I chew my lip as I rinse the suds from my hair.

There's no sign of a woman in the apartment. Nothing noticeably feminine. It's simple. Concise. Orderly. And very masculine. Strange. Unless he prefers to wash his longish hair with something more effective than bar soap?

What other mysteries does Claude keep hidden? It seems there's more to him than meets the eye. My curiosity increases at the thought of unraveling complex layers beneath his stoic exterior.

The kindness of this one-armed bartender brought me here. Ensured my safety. And I shouldn't pry into his personal life. I'm a guest, however temporary, and should keep my nosy inquiries to myself.

Still, his immediate instinct to protect me leaves me in a soft, mushy place. He's handsome, though not in a traditional way, and radiates an appeal that goes beyond looks. His wavy dark hair, his soft brown eyes, his nose that should be too long but is somehow balanced in proportion to his face and height.

Part of me wonders how he would look in a tuxedo on my arm at a gala. I shake my head. He would be out of place at such an event. Here, behind the bar, wearing a dark plaid shirt, rock band tee shirt, and jeans—that's his element. I'm sure of it.

I finish showering and dry off before realizing I don't have anything to sleep in. Gathering the discarded garments from the floor, I return to the bedroom.

It hits me.

There's only one bed.

One. Bed.

The thought warms me. He never said anything about where *he* was going to sleep. He's not going to sleep on the sofa, is he? With his height and broad shoulders, that can't be comfortable.

I glance at the queen-size bed with its tidy blankets and cozy pillows. Longing strikes me. But I can't put him out in his own home.

I'll let him have the bed. I'll take the sofa.

That's when I spot the pile of clothes on the bed. I pick up the shirt and unfold it. No letters or words, just deep blue fabric. I hold it close, inhaling a subtle scent of detergent and something musky I assume belongs solely to Claude. When I slip the clothes on, they cradle me like a warm blanket, soothing my world-weary heart and restoring my faith in humanity.

After folding and placing the other clothes on the dresser, I open the door to the living room.

Claude's stretched out on the sofa, his feet hanging off the end and his eyes closed. Nothing about his position looks comfortable. How can he possibly sleep like that?

"Do you need something?" he asks, keeping his eyes closed.

"No, but..." I step closer and rest my hand on the back of

the couch. "I can sleep on the couch…"

He peers up at me, those kind eyes fixing on my face, and it's almost as if he's taking measure of me. "I'm fine here. You take the bed."

"You don't look comfortable." I gesture to his feet dangling well past the end of the sofa. "This couch is far too small for you."

"It won't be the first time I've slept here, and I doubt it'll be the last." He shifts, folding his arms across his chest. "Take the bed. I'll be fine."

I twist the hem of my shirt between my fingers. "We could share the bed…"

He narrows his eyes, and I feel like I'm under a microscope as he studies me.

"I don't think that would be a good idea."

"I don't bite. I promise." A grin splits my lips, but it dissolves at the thought of his long limbs wrapped around me in the comfort of his bed. Warmth infuses me, flooding my cheeks.

"I don't think your fiancé would appreciate you sharing a bed with another man." He exhales sharply. "Just spending the night here is pushing it."

Disappointment fills me, and I bite back a retort. I want to tell him exactly how little I care what my *ex*-fiancé thinks of where I sleep. "Do you want me to leave?"

"No."

He answers so quickly, it gives me hope I'm not about to be kicked out into the storm.

"I don't want to be a bother. I'll leave."

When I turn away, Claude sighs and climbs to his feet. "Gwen."

His voice echoes behind me, and I turn around to face him. The moment our eyes meet, I feel that pull between us again.

"I'm sorry. I don't mean to be a burden."

"You're not a burden." He runs his fingers through his hair. "I just…I'm bad at this."

"Bad at what?"

"Playing the hero. Talking to beautiful women. Take your

pick."

My heart beats faster. "You think I'm beautiful?"

He clears his throat and drops his gaze. The muscles in his neck work as he tries to formulate a response. When he looks up, his whiskey eyes sparkle in the dim light. "Please take the bed. I'm trying to be a gentleman."

"You don't have to try, Claude." I beam at him. "You're the only true gentleman I've ever met."

His lips thin into a line, and his cheeks flush pink. "Good night, Gwen."

I refrain from touching him, afraid he'll spontaneously combust at the contact. "Good night, Claude."

Without pressing the issue further, I slip around him and disappear into the bedroom, leaving the door cracked open. I turn off the light and crawl into his bed.

I nestle into the pillow, inhaling deeply. His scent surrounds me. The mild detergent and Irish Spring linger, but there's no denying the scent of *him* beneath it all. Spice and leather with the warmth of cinnamon.

No coconut. Interesting.

My eyes grow heavy as warmth surrounds my body, pulling me under until exhaustion finally closes my eyes. The sliver of light through the door draws me like a moth to a flame.

I wish he would have taken me up on my offer to share. I'm tired of being alone.

CHAPTER FIVE
CLAUDE

I've slept better on a jungle hillside in a torrential downpour.

After cursing the aging sofa and my vivid imagination, I manage to steal a few hours of restless sleep. These couch springs should be classified as torture devices. I really need to get rid of it, buy something new. Something that won't stab me in my sleep.

But I can't completely blame the couch for my lack of rest. That fault lays firmly at the feet of the woman passed out blissfully in my bed at this moment. I thought the image of her naked in my shower would haunt me well into morning, but it was the invitation to join her in my bed that gave me a demanding hard-on and no peace.

I shouldn't be thinking about her like that. She's not mine, and judging by the expensive clothes and shitty fiancé, she never will be. Still, I wonder what she's hiding and why she's going to such lengths to run from her problems.

At daybreak, I concede defeat and get up. There will be no rest with her in my home. I can't purge thoughts of her long enough to fall asleep. Just knowing she's curled up, safe and warm in my bed, leaves my whole body aching for release.

I slip into the bedroom to grab some clothes. She's asleep, her back to me, blankets over her head. Careful not to make too much noise, I retrieve the clothes and tiptoe into the bathroom, closing the door softly behind me. Once I've showered and dressed, I return to the living room through the other door.

Frost cakes the windows and snow piles on the ledges, making it difficult to see the streets below. At least it's stopped snowing. Not that it matters. In a day or two, the snow will melt, leaving a mess of slush and mud coating the streets and sidewalks. This storm caught us all off-guard. It's not common to have this much snow in the first week of December. I'll have to replace the mat by the front door to catch the slop.

Exhaustion lingers, and I yawn as I set the coffee pot to brew. I grab a carton of eggs and some cheese from the refrigerator. There isn't a lot of variety in my pantry—I eat most of my meals in the bar—but there are always ingredients for cheese omelets here. They're a kind of comfort food for me.

I crack the eggs and whisk them in a bowl as the skillet warms, a tablespoon of butter melting in the center. I smile at the satisfying sizzle of eggs as I gently mix them while they cook. I turn the heat to low and let them sit. A sprinkle of cheese, and I pull them from the heat. Then I repeat the process, making an omelet for my guest without a second thought.

"Something smells delicious." Her voice, rough with sleep, pulls me from my silent motions.

"Good morning. Hope you're hungry."

"Starving." She takes the plate I've offered and retreats to the small table.

I finish cooking my own eggs and grab two forks from the drawer beside the sink. "Here." I hand her a fork and set my plate down. "Do you want some coffee?"

"Yes, please."

After I pour us both a cup of rich coffee, I turn. She's sitting with one knee folded beneath her. The worn material of my old shirt is stretched, exposing a creamy shoulder. She looks like a fairy princess relaxing beside a pool in a painting I can't quite place. Shaking the thought free, I hand her a mug.

She accepts it gratefully and inhales the aroma with a moan of delight.

I sit, painfully aware of the effect her presence has on my body. She's pure temptation. My clothes hug her curves in all the right places. Just knowing she's wearing them leaves me aching with a possessive need I've never felt before. I want to know what lies beneath the familiar fabric.

"Thank you." She takes a bite of the omelet and sighs. "This is delicious."

"Glad you like it." I poke at my eggs, my hunger replaced by something carnal. I manage to stuff a few bites in my mouth, and the motion nudges me to continue eating.

"You like to read?" she asks, gesturing to the bookshelf along the far wall.

"Yeah, when I get time."

"The bar keeps you busy?"

"It does, but I like it. Makes me feel productive."

She smiles, and my reservations melt.

"How long have you been a bartender?"

"Since 1973…so twelve years." I sip my coffee. "My grandfather owned the place. Taught me everything he knew before he let me take over."

"He must be very proud of you."

"He was." I clear my throat. "The building takes a lot of work, the bar even more. I feel like I'm constantly fixing something."

"I can imagine. They've got a lot of character though. The building. The bar."

"A lot of history here." Memories dance in the back of my mind. "Takes hard work to preserve them."

"And money," she says softly. When she meets my gaze again, she brightens. "What's your favorite Shakespeare play?"

I laugh, marveling at the way she bounces from one topic to another. "*Much Ado About Nothing.*"

"Ahh, so you're a romantic."

Her teasing observation plucks my heartstrings.

"I've been called worse."

We continue to eat amid friendly conversation, and I like it. Her presence adds something unique and unfamiliar to my routine. The little bit of time I spent in Quinn's company a few months ago reminded me how much I miss the companionship of another soul. I've lived with roommates before, particularly during my time in the Army, but I've never shared my space— or my life—with a woman. I've always been terrified I'm going to say or do something stupid. With Gwen, that fear has vanished.

When she finishes her breakfast, she takes her plate to the sink and returns for mine. I sip my coffee in silence as she washes the dishes and sets them in the drying rack. Her question from the night before emerges in the front of my brain. "You really want to work at the bar?" I set the empty mug aside.

She spins around and nods. "Yes."

I rise from the table and grab my flannel shirt from a hook by the door. "Get dressed and come downstairs."

"I'll be right down." Gwen flashes me a smile and darts back into the bedroom.

My body protests every step as I descend the aging staircase. In all the years I've owned this place, I've never felt the need to make improvements or turn it into something it's not, and I've been remiss in updating the bar and the apartments above it. I've always just done basic maintenance to keep it functional, not stylish. Now that Quinn and Grant are always home on the second floor, I feel pressure to be a better landlord. I make a mental note to call Jack and have him start doing some work on the building. Pap left enough money to ensure that kind of stuff was taken care of. Old buildings deteriorate and need love. At least that's what I'm telling myself. My desire to improve the place has nothing to do with the curvy brunette who's wedged herself into my life.

She's not staying. I need to remember that.

The Black Penny is exactly how I left it the night before. I turn on the lights and flip the on switch for the jukebox in the corner. The bright colors illuminate the space. I'm home.

From behind the polished wooden surface of the bar, I pull out a variety of glasses. If Gwen is serious about working for me, she needs to prove she understands the basics. Any bar owner worth their salt should ensure the staff knows how to work behind the bar first. Everything else is easy.

"What time do you open?"

When I turn, Gwen is standing by the swinging doors, just over the edge of the tile.

"Five on a Sunday. Four every other day of the week. I used

to be closed on Mondays, but people need a refuge."

She comes alongside me, eyeing the glasses. "What's this for?"

"Bartending 101."

"Is there a test?"

"This whole thing is a test." I lean against a shelf beside the register. "Pass it and you got the job. Fail it and…" I shrug my shoulder in a carefree way and leave the consequence unspoken.

"Okay." She takes a deep breath.

"What types of glasses are these?"

"This is a martini glass. This is for beer. That's for wine. Oh, that's a champagne glass." Her nose scrunches as she goes down the line. "Whiskey?" Defeat rings in her tone when she reaches a tall one. "I don't know."

"That's a highball glass." I point to the one that stumped her then move to the one she called a whiskey glass. "This is a rocks glass."

"Oh yeah." She bites her lip.

"Not bad." I shift closer and put all but two glasses away.

She stares at the martini and the rocks glasses left on the bar.

"Now for the true test. Make a Manhattan and a dirty gin martini with two olives."

She blinks at me like a stray cat caught in cab headlights. "What?"

"The couple who just came in wants a dirty gin martini with two olives and a Manhattan. I'm busy in the kitchen. You need to make the drinks without my help."

Tentatively, she searches the shelves for the gin. When she pulls a vodka bottle, I stop her and show her how the bar is laid out and where to find the proper ingredients. It's pretty simple with everything on display. I can tell she's nervous when the bottle nearly slips from her hand.

"Easy, darlin'." I grab the bottle before it crashes to the floor. "Why don't we take it a little slower?"

She nods in relief. "Yes, please."

I set the bottle aside and hand her a small metal container

with all my drink recipes in it. I haven't used it in years, but every one of my employees starts with it and uses these recipes until they're comfortable on their own.

"Why don't you look here for the recipes, then try your hand at making the two I requested?" I turn to get my weekly checklist for liquor and food orders.

"Thank you for teaching me, Claude."

Her sweet words tug at my heart.

With a nod, I clear my throat. "I'll let you practice. Yell if you need anything."

Her plump lower lip disappears between her teeth, and she nods enthusiastically before turning back to the bar and opening the recipe catalog.

I run through my list, painfully aware of her warm presence behind me. I'm asking for trouble with this temporary solution, aren't I? This wayward kitten already has a home, and heartache is a foregone conclusion.

Being nice always leads to heartache.

CHAPTER SIX
GWEN

The silence is too much. I feel like I'm drifting alone in the open sea, cut off from everyone and everything.

My gaze drifts around the empty bar and rests longingly on the jukebox. A little music would lighten my mood. I pat my empty pockets. No money. Damn.

Taking the little recipe box with me, I go to the other side of the bar and sit on a bench. The recipes are organized alphabetically, so I start with A and work my way through the catalog. The faint strains of a rock ballad play in my head while I read. I hum along as I skim the ingredients and instructions, and then set each card aside, keeping them in order.

I'm about halfway through the stack of recipes when Claude appears from the kitchen. He stalks across the room, drops some coins in the jukebox, and selects a song.

The strains I've been playing in my head come through the speakers. I bounce my foot with the beat and sing along. The music wraps around me, soothing me in ways I didn't realize I needed. The catchy beat fills the room, and suddenly, I don't feel alone anymore.

I shoot Claude a grateful smile when he returns. "Thanks, it was too quiet in here."

"It won't be once we open." He pauses in the doorway. "How's it going?"

"Good."

"Any questions so far?"

"No." I fan the cards in my hand, seeing how many I have left. "I hope you don't expect me to memorize all of these."

"I don't." He chuckles. "But it's good to be familiar with them."

"Yeah."

"You ready to try a few yet?"

"Almost." I hold up what remains of the deck.

"As soon as you're ready, you can show me what you've learned."

He vanishes into the hallway, leaving me to my own devices.

I spend another ten minutes reading the recipes. Confidence fills me, even though there are terms I'm not quite sure of written in the instructions. What does it mean to *muddle?* What the hell is a *jigger?* What makes a dirty martini *dirty?* I mentally file these questions away. Once Claude comes back, I can ask him to clarify.

Pushing aside my apprehension, I return the recipes to the box and set it on the bar before venturing into the kitchen in search of Claude. He's taking inventory in the small walk-in freezer.

"I'm ready." My confidence takes a hit at his skeptical expression. I note the tension in his jaw as he finishes a note on his checklist.

He leads me back to the bar and sets the list aside. "Well then. Let's see you make something."

"What do you want?" I turn and smile.

His brow furrows for a moment, but it smooths instantly as he leans against the bar. "Let's start with the Manhattan."

I reach for the cards on the counter and pull out the one for the drink he requested. After a quick scan of the ingredients, I retrieve the whiskey, bitters, and sweet vermouth. When I reach for a rocks glass, he clicks his tongue.

I consider my options, then frown. "Is this a trick question?"

"Feels like it, doesn't it?" He takes out both a highball and a martini glass. "On the rocks," he says, pointing at the tall slender glass before moving to the martini glass. "No rocks."

"Rocks? That's a silly name for ice." I chuckle. "Let's make it on the rocks."

He watches silently as I take the mixing glass and search for a way to measure the liquor. His groan rips through me when I try to pour freehand.

"You're not ready for that yet, sweetheart." He grabs the liquor bottle and what looks like a small, uneven hourglass. Standing next to me, he pauses to make sure my full attention is on him. Where else would it be? His mere presence makes it hard to focus on anything *but* him.

"What's that?" I point to the hourglass thingy in his massive hand, ignoring the heat creeping along my neck at his close proximity.

"This is a jigger." He shows me the big end. "Two ounces." He flips it. "One ounce." Holding it between his fingers, he empties the haphazardly poured whiskey from the cup into the big end before deftly transferring it to the waiting empty glass. Then he measures the vermouth with the small end. He dashes a few drops from a small, awkwardly wrapped bottle into the mix. "Don't forget the ice." He pours a small scoop of ice into the glass and stirs it with a tall, red-tipped spoon.

"Make sure it's mixed properly, then add a cherry on top." He does so and slides the glass toward me. "Always wash your utensils after making a drink." Claude nods at the small sink by my hip.

"Can I try it?" At his nod, I sip the Manhattan. The burn of whiskey is dulled by sweet vermouth, and it has a bitter aftertaste. I scrunch up my nose and set it aside.

Claude chuckles. "Not your style, huh?"

"No. I liked the drink you made for me last night."

"Do you want to learn how to make it?" His smile widens as he reaches for the gin on the shelf behind him.

"Yes, please." My excitement bubbles up.

Step-by-step, Claude walks me through the process. I watch with fascination as he grinds rosemary leaves and cucumber with simple syrup at the bottom of a glass. He uses the word muddle, and a puzzle piece fits into place when I make the connection. Then he adds the liquor, gives it a shake, and strains it into a fancy glass.

"You make it look so simple." I pick up the glass and savor the refreshing cocktail. It may be only ten in the morning, but I deserve a treat.

"There's nothing to it." He shrugs and replaces the bottles. "Just practice."

His arm brushes mine as he reaches past me. Heat surrounds me, followed by the teasing whiff of his scent. A scent that's familiar and comforting. One that tormented me all night. It clings to my skin after sleeping in his bed, wearing his clothes. I lean into his path as he passes and inhale deeply. His back is turned, and I sigh in frustration when he steps away.

Claude gives me a quick introduction to the tools of his trade. He probably should have started here. I have no idea if he was testing me or challenging me, but it would have helped to know these things before I dove into making dirty martinis or fancy whiskey drinks.

When he finishes, he lapses into silence as he cleans the few dishes we used. I want to ask him more about himself, but he doesn't seem very talkative when he's not teaching me some tidbit or giving instruction.

The gin fizzles through me, sparking my bravery. I come up beside him and sway against him, nudging his thigh with my hip. "How come you don't drink?"

"Doesn't sit well with me." He dries a glass and sets it aside.

"Someone made you a bad drink?"

"Nope." He sighs. "Just gave it up when it hurt more than it helped."

"That makes sense." I study his profile as he works. "I'm sure you didn't always want to be a bartender."

"You'd be right."

"What did you want to be?" I sip my drink.

"A cop."

"Really?" I stare at him, surprised.

"Yeah, but after the war…" He raises his left arm with the absent hand. "I didn't quite meet the requirements."

I'm struck by the sadness in his tone.

"Is that how you lost your arm? The war?" I ask, my voice soft. Maybe I'm not supposed to ask such a question, but curiosity, emboldened by alcohol, increases my desperation to know.

"Yeah, but I didn't lose my whole arm." He pushes his hair back from his face. "I lost my hand and part of my forearm. Not that it matters. It was enough to ruin my job prospects."

Tears prick my eyes. All my life, I've been locked in my family's gilded apartments, toured the most elegant establishments, eaten the finest meals. I can't even make my own fucking drink, but this sweet, selfless man sacrificed so much in service to his country. I feel like a spoiled brat complaining about my problems. We're from separate worlds with completely different experiences. The gap between us is wide, but I'm determined to bridge it.

"Well, you're a damn good bartender." I rest my hand on his shoulder.

His eyes brighten and fix on me. "What did you want to be?"

"Free." The word slips out before I can stop it.

I shake my head and chuckle, trying to cover my mistake, but it's too late. The word is out there, floating on the air like dandelion fluff. He doesn't say anything, even though I can feel his curious gaze studying me.

"I mean, I always wanted to have my own place, maybe have a shop somewhere, selling jewelry or custom goods."

"Hmm." He turns back to his task.

I don't think he believes me. "I bet you get a lot of ladies in here."

Claude turns to me, confusion etched along his handsome face. "Why do you say that?"

"Come on…you're a handsome guy, with those soulful eyes and that charming smile."

His brow furrows as he ponders my words.

I warm under the tension, thinking I said something wrong.

When he finally speaks, his voice is rough. "Do you do that often?"

"Do what?"

"Flirt to redirect the conversation?"

I gasp at his question. "I…uh…no." I clear my throat. "I

was just curious about why a good-looking guy like you is still single."

"As you can tell by the absence of a line of women around the block, no one wants a broken, one-armed bartender."

I do. A small, persistent part of my brain screams at the top of its lungs.

There's pain in his eyes. A pain I can relate to at a level most others can't even imagine.

"I understand."

My voice stops him, and he regards me like a hound with big eyes and floppy ears.

"It would be nice to be desired for what I am on the inside instead of for my looks or connections or what my family can give. I'm constantly rejected for my passions, my heart…hell, even my inexperience in the world outside my sheltered existence has left me with horrible self-confidence. I am an impostor among my peers."

I just want to be loved. The last sentence nearly strangles me. I shrug, thinking I went too far, revealed too much.

"I'm sorry, Gwen." Claude rakes his hand through his hair. "People can be assholes. Don't let it steal your sparkle though. You've still got some." His smile leaves me breathless.

"I doubt that," I mumble under my breath before pasting on a fake smile. I'm not sure I believe him. I've been reminded often how useless I really am. How stupid my dreams are. I'm half afraid I believe the lies.

"Keep studying. You'll figure it out," Claude says, turning away. "I'll be back in a few. If you need me, I'll be in the office." He retreats, taking his checklist with him.

Once again, I'm alone, left to wonder if I crossed a line by opening my big mouth. Shit. I thought we were getting to know each other. It's hard not to take it personally when you're desperate for some kind of connection.

I grab the cards and skim through them again, losing myself in the recipes, trying to focus on something other than the gentle pull of his presence and his kind words.

Don't let it steal your sparkle.

I'll try, Claude. I'll try.

CHAPTER SEVEN
CLAUDE

Even within the confines of my office, she haunts me. Working beside her could be dangerous. She's temptation incarnate, with a body made for sin and a smile that rivals a summer sunrise over the bay.

I collapse into my chair and toss the order sheets on the desk. What the hell am I doing? I'm tormenting myself. Honestly, I don't need the distraction of her in the bar every day. We haven't even discussed her living arrangements. Not that I'll be quick to throw her out in the street. She can stay with me as long as she needs to. As long as it takes to find a place of her own.

But having her in my life on a daily basis will only lead to heartache. I can see it coming a mile away.

With a groan, I lean back and close my eyes, stretching my aching back. Sleeping on the sofa didn't help, but I've slept in worse places under worse conditions. Crashing on the old worn couch my grandfather left behind won't be the death of me.

Gwen might be though.

Grabbing the phone, I dial the number for the courier my brother uses to deliver things across town. With a few quick instructions and payment arranged, I schedule the pickup for an hour from now. I'll pay for the quick turnaround, but I promised Marcy I'd have the gown in her hands today.

After I hang up, I stare at the bloodstained dress, wrapped discreetly in a small black garbage bag on the corner of my desk. I scribble a note with the name and address and tape it to the bag, ensuring it's firmly tied closed before pushing it aside.

The questions resurface in the back of my mind. Who is she? And what the hell happened between her and her fiancé last night?

It's really none of my business. I did my duty and stepped between them when she asked. Judging from the look of the guy who barged into my place demanding answers, I'd guess he didn't have her best interests at heart. And if she hit him, he deserved it. Best keep a little distance between them for the moment.

But the truth creeps in like ink spilled into crystal-clear water. He'll be back. And she'll have to face him.

Hell, maybe she'll want him back at that point. I don't know. I shouldn't care.

I *don't* care. It's her life. She can do what she wants.

Then why the hell am I sticking my neck out for her? Letting her stay with me? Hiring her to work at the bar? This is a guaranteed disaster waiting to happen.

The moment her fiancé shows up and shit goes south, I'll be caught in it. When she chooses him, whatever high I'm drifting on will be ripped out from under me and bring me crashing to earth.

I know the type. Entitled, indecisive. They sink their claws into people, use them, throw them away the moment something better comes along. I *can't* let her get under my skin. I have too much at stake—my business, my simple life. I won't let a beautiful stranger waltz in and rip it all away without a shred of remorse.

But is that truly who she is?

That's how people born with money are. I've met enough rich bastards to know they're only along for the ride while it's all ups. The moment things take a turn, they bail. They don't care who they ruin in the process.

A mental picture of Gwen in the blood-covered gown, shivering and desperate, pops into my mind. It's hard to believe she could be so cold and callous, but I actually know nothing about her. She refuses to share details. I get it. She'll tell me when she's ready, but damn if my curiosity isn't wearing a hole in my brain with the constant burning questions.

I want to respect her privacy. Maybe one day she'll trust me with her story, maybe not. But whatever trouble she's wrapped up in, she's tangled me in it too. She's clammed up and scared, which says enough. The girl is hiding something. I just wish she'd trust me.

The phone rings, jerking me from my thoughts. "Black Penny."

"Claude, what are you doing in the office on a Sunday?" My brother's voice booms through the line.

"Inventory, Grant, like I do every Sunday." I lean back in the chair.

"That's right. I forgot you're married to the bar." He pulls away from the phone, and I hear him mumbling to Quinn, his girlfriend. "You still coming for dinner tonight?"

Damn it. In all the commotion, I forgot about Sunday family dinner. There's no way I can skip it or force Gwen to stay home alone. "Yeah, I think there's enough help to cover the bar tonight. We'll be there."

"We?" Grant picks out the one piece of information that doesn't quite fit. That's what detectives do best.

I curse the slip of my tongue, but it doesn't matter, he'd find out about her sooner or later. Better get it over with now. "Yeah, I have someone staying with me. Mind if she comes?"

"She?" His interest is piqued. "Who is *she?*"

"You'll meet her later. Now can I finish my inventory?"

"Sure."

"Oh, does Quinn have some clothes she can borrow?"

Grant chuckles. "Did she show up naked on your doorstep?"

My gaze lands on the bag containing her bloody gown. "Not exactly. I'll explain later."

"All right. I'll have Quinn bring some clothes down to the office."

"Just have her put them in front of my door. We need to change before we come over."

"I'm sure you do." Grant's tone brims with amusement.

I'll be bombarded with a thousand questions during dinner. I should probably warn Gwen before I drag her into the lion's den.

"See you then." I hang up without waiting for my brother's response.

The buzzer at the side door rings. I had it installed for deliveries and emergencies after the whole mess with Quinn a few months ago. Grabbing the bag, I head down the hall and open the door. A chilly gust bursts through the door and stings my skin, even through my warm flannel shirt.

"Afternoon, sir." The young man's breath curls in the cold air. The snow is melting into slush, but he's wearing boots and a warm winter coat. Beneath the wool cap, he flashes a smile.

"Hope you're staying warm." I hand him the parcel. He takes it in his mittened hand and tucks it beneath his arm. "Cold one today."

"That it is, sir." He nods.

"Address is on the package." I give him a generous tip. "Be quick about it, please."

"Of course, sir. Have a good one."

After he leaves, I close and lock the door. Hopefully, Marcy will be able to take care of the stains. Gwen looked amazing in that gown. I would hate to have it permanently tarnished due to her fiancé's incompetence as a decent human being.

When I return to the bar, Foreigner's "I Wanna Know What Love Is" plays over the speakers. I lean against the wall, remaining in the shadows, mesmerized by the sight before me.

Gwen is dancing in the middle of the bar, her arms moving with the beat, her hair swaying behind her like a dark veil. It takes me a moment to realize she's singing along. Her sweet voice fills the empty space.

My heart constricts. How could something so beautiful be so damned tempting? Or unattainable?

She's out of my league. Even in the old sweatshirt I loaned her, she looks like a goddess here to torment mortal men. Or maybe an elf.

I shake my head. I've been reading too much Tolkien. Maybe I should stick to Stephen King. At least there's no gilded temptation there.

Gwen spins around and stops when she sees me step into view. "Sorry. I just love this song. It makes me want to dance."

Her breathless laugh sends a bolt of need through me.

"We all have those moments." I clear my throat. "Would you be interested in joining me for dinner at my brother's?"

She blinks up at me with those luminous, intoxicating eyes. When she smiles, a small crease forms at the corners, charming and carefree. "You want me to come with you to dinner with your family?"

"Well, it's not my *whole* family. It's just my brother and his girlfriend. They live on the second fl—."

"I'd love to." Her smile fades, and she tugs at the hem of her sweatshirt. "But what will I wear?"

"Quinn has some clothes you can borrow."

"Quinn?"

"My brother's girlfriend." I motion for her to follow me. "Come on."

Gwen bounds over and rises on her tiptoes to kiss my cheek. "Thank you, Claude. You think of everything."

The warmth of her lips brands me. It takes all my effort to not drag her against me so I can discover just how soft and pliant her lips are under mine. My cock twitches as she disappears down the hallway.

I thought of everything, all right. That's why I'm mired in this mess, up to my old, lonely heart.

CHAPTER EIGHT
GWEN

I tug at the sleeves of the borrowed sweater and struggle to relax. *It's only dinner with his family.*

But what if they ask questions I'm unprepared to answer? I don't want to get them involved. It's better if they don't know who I am.

Right? Indecision claws at me, and I bite my lip as thoughts race through my head.

Claude knocks on his brother's apartment door, then glances at me. "Are you okay?"

"Fine," I lie, flashing a halfhearted smile.

"They won't bite, I promise." He returns the smile.

Warmth radiates through me. How did I end up in the company of such a sweet man? All my life, I've lived in fear of the men around me. Their power. Their status. Their influence. Their lust. It's surreal to be with a man who isn't expecting anything from me…from us. I step closer, soaking up his heat, longing to be near him.

The door swings open, and I blink in surprise when Claude's brother steps into view. They're so similar, they could be twins. Claude's hair is longer and his demeanor more relaxed, but they have the same facial structure and dark features.

"Gwen, this is my brother Grant."

I shake myself from a stupor and take his hand. "Nice to meet you," I say, keeping my voice steady.

"Likewise." Grant opens the door wider and invites us inside.

I follow Claude into the apartment. Its layout is nearly identical to Claude's, but there's a distinct difference in décor and mood. Bright fabrics cover the sofa, a plush carpet brightens the dark space, and a bookcase filled with books lines the far wall.

"Dinner will be ready in a minute."

I spin around to see a gorgeous, curvy redhead wearing a green apron. She places a covered dish on a small table with four place settings. Her curls cascade in a mass over her shoulder. She turns with a smile, and I'm stunned by how lovely she is. And young. She can't be much older than twenty-four.

But looks can be deceiving…I should know. I hide the fact I'm twenty-five with a thick layer of makeup and the latest fashion trends. We're similar in body type, which makes sense considering her clothes fit me perfectly.

"That's Quinn." Claude comes alongside me. "My brother's girlfriend."

"Oh." I turn to see Grant limp toward her. He presses a kiss to her forehead and sits at the table. "What happened to him?" I whisper, curiosity tugging at the threads in my mind.

"He was shot a few months ago. Still recovering."

"Shot?" I gasp. "How?"

"It's a long story, but it's a risk a homicide detective takes."

"He's a cop?" Uncertainty tightens deep in my chest. This could complicate everything, especially if my family files a missing person's report.

"Yeah, but he's on leave while he recovers." Claude motions for me to join them at the table.

Slowly, the knot in my chest unravels. There's no threat here. It's just a family meal. Nothing sinister or underhanded.

Not like it would be under my father's roof.

Quinn pauses and offers her hand. "I'm so glad you're here." She beams. "It'll be refreshing to not hear them argue through the whole meal. You'll balance things out."

"Thank you for inviting me on such short notice." I take the seat opposite her. Tension zings down my spine at the intimacy of such an informal dinner. I can't remember the last time I had a casual meal with my family…or anyone else for that matter. Meals were always a production in my home. I hated them with a passion.

The brothers fall into a conversation about some court case

blowing up the news. Quinn fills my plate. Pot roast, mashed potatoes, mixed vegetables. It all looks delicious. I take a few bites as the animated discussion between Claude and Grant continues.

Claude's attention drifts to me, even as his brother speaks. I smile, and the corner of his mouth quirks.

"So, Gwen, how did you meet Claude?" Quinn cuts through their conversation, obviously disinterested in it.

Claude chokes on a piece of roast beef and takes a drink of his water.

"Oh…well…" I search for the proper response.

"She came into the bar last night," Claude says. "Had some trouble and needed a place to stay."

Grant chews thoughtfully, his gaze searching me. I can't tell what's going on in his head, but Quinn interjects before I can think too much about it.

"You're such a sweetheart, Claude, coming to her aid like that." She rests her hand on his shoulder.

"He always was the sentimental kind," Grant grumbles under his breath. "Dad nearly had a fit when he brought home strays as a kid. But it never stopped him."

I bristle at his insinuation. Me? Is he comparing *me* to an abandoned pet? Warmth floods my cheeks. Thinking about the dynamics in my family, he's not far off.

"She's not a stray cat." Quinn shakes her finger at him. "And don't forget, you took me in when I needed help."

"Don't remind me." He flinches as she gently shoves his shoulder.

A smile breaks his stony expression, and my heart flips at the look they share.

They're in love. Absolutely head over heels. Smitten. Jealousy pierces my heart. What I wouldn't give to have someone look at me in such a tender way.

"How did you two meet?" I ask, curious about the romance playing out in front of me.

Quinn's face turns pink, and she clears her throat. "Well, that's a complicated story—"

"I caught her stealing shit that didn't belong to her." Grant stabs a piece of meat. "Two months later, she showed up on my doorstep with stab wounds, as a murder witness."

My fork clatters to the plate. "You…what?"

"Like I said, it's complicated." Quinn chuckles and lifts her glass in salute before taking a drink.

"How long are you staying with my brother?" Grant changes the topic.

I glance at Claude, who seems unbothered by the conversation's abrupt detour.

"She's welcome to stay as long as she needs to."

My heart swells. "Thank you."

Quinn shifts the conversation again, moving to lighter topics. I can't help but feel a twinge of jealousy at what she has with Grant. Their love is potent, obvious in every line shared, every glance, every smile. Even with their difference in age, I can see how much they care for each other, how they're in harmony with one another.

In all my life, I've never seen such unabashed adoration between two people. My parents didn't marry for love. It was a business transaction. Everything they did was for power and status. For show. And I am expected to play my part in an ongoing performance by marrying a man I loathe.

Throughout the meal, I'm haunted by thoughts of my past and the dread hanging over my head. I do my best to ignore the pressure from their weight, but seeing what I've been missing leaves an ache deep in my chest.

After dinner, I help Quinn clean the dishes. She's funny and full of energy. We laugh as we discuss the latest films and music. She has an affinity for Stephen King, like Claude, and enjoys movies, from classic films to modern action flicks. I like her already. In a different life, we could have been best friends.

I'll take these sweet kernels of friendship. These stolen moments of joy give me hope that there's something out there for me, beyond my family and their oppressive grip on my life.

Claude and Grant sip coffee at the table. I steal a glance at them and admire Claude's profile. Warmth surrounds me. I wonder whether his lips are as soft as they look. Do they taste like the apple pie we had for dessert?

Quinn nudges me with her hip. "Penny for your thoughts?" she asks, her voice low.

My face warms. "Oh, nothing."

"You can't fool me, honey." She grins. "I've seen that look before. Hell, I've worn it."

"I don't know what you're talking about." I dry the plate in my hands and set it in the cabinet.

"Mm-hmm." Quinn sighs. "Well, between you and me, Claude could use a distraction. He lives at the bar. It's his whole life."

"Isn't that a good thing? He has something he loves."

"Some*one* would be better." She sets aside the last plate and leans against the counter. "He's been alone for too long. It's nice to see him interested in something other than his work or his books."

My face heats at the implication of her words. She thinks there's something going on between Claude and me. I don't want to ruin her hope by correcting her, and I allow myself to imagine what it would be like to be with him.

"Are you ready to go?" Claude asks, breaking into my thoughts.

I jump and spin around. "Yes, I'm ready."

We exchange goodbyes, and Quinn hugs me tight. "Let me know if you need anything. I'll be here, taking care of the old man."

"I heard that." Grant grabs her by the waist and pulls her against him. "Nice to meet you, Gwen."

"Thanks again for dinner." I wave and follow Claude into the hallway.

When we reach his apartment, he lets me enter the room first, then closes the door behind us. My body thrums just being in his presence. Can he feel it too? I can't be the only one. I've felt more love in this place in the past two days than I've ever felt over the duration of my entire life.

"Did you enjoy yourself?"

Tears prick my eyes. "I did." I hastily wipe them away, hoping he doesn't see.

"Then why are you crying?" He steps closer and brushes his thumb across my cheek, catching a few stray tears.

I sway toward him at the tender gesture. "My family isn't nearly as welcoming as yours." I lift my chin to meet his gaze. "You're lucky to have them in your life." I sniff as the tears flow.

Claude embraces me, wrapping his one arm tight around my waist. His heat surrounds me, and I bury my face against the warm flannel of his shirt. He smells so good. Like spices and soap. The subtle aroma of *him* beneath it all unleashes a need inside me. I cling to his shirt until the sobs subside. When I finally feel grounded again, I lean back and wipe my face with my hand.

"Sorry about that." I laugh softly. "Thank you for everything."

When I press a kiss to his cheek, he goes still. I pull back, my lips hovering near his mouth. His eyes are closed, his lower lip trembling.

"Gwen." He opens his eyes, and deep in their dark centers, I can see hunger. Need.

Even though I want more than he may be willing to give— more than I have to offer—I refuse to ignore the tension simmering between us for a moment longer.

I take the chance and close the gap between us. My lips meet his, his goatee brushing my skin, and I kiss him softly. Reverently. With no expectation.

CHAPTER NINE
CLAUDE

Sweet merciful God. Am I dead?

I inhale sharply, taking the sweet scent of her deep into my lungs, my heart constricting. Her kiss catches me with an unsteady right hook. The press of her lips sends an electric pulse through me. My hand grips her waist. She leans into the touch, pressing her body to mine.

There's no part of her I wouldn't explore. Every delicious curve tucked against me drives my hunger deeper. She tastes like apples and cloves. A groan rips from my throat when she wraps her arms around my neck and buries her fingers in my hair.

Her gentle touch against my nape unleashes my restraint. I pull her toward me and slant my mouth over hers. She opens, and I'm lost in her glittering web.

When she walked into my bar, she shone with a brilliance I'd never seen before. Even in her blood-soaked gown, wearing tearstains like a badge of honor, she looked regal. A diamond shining in the darkness.

But now she fucking glows, brighter than the North Star.

She tugs my hair as I delve deeper, tasting her mouth, exploring her with equal parts curiosity and enthusiasm. Her gasping breaths mirror my own.

It's been years since I've kissed a woman, felt the heat of her surging through my blood. My body hums with desperate, clumsy emotions coursing through me. I want her. More than I should. She wants me, and I'm dumbfounded at the realization.

"Claude," she murmurs against my mouth, grinding her hips on my thigh. "I won't break if you touch me."

My fingers tighten on her waist. A slight shift of my hand and I could delve beneath the fabric of her shirt, feel the delicate skin I've been dying to explore.

She threads her fingers through my hair and pulls hard enough to force my head back.

Our eyes lock. The blue captures me, swirling in an endless sea. I want to surrender to the plea I see swimming in their depths. She wants me to make love to her.

But as much as I long to bury myself deep inside her, I won't. I can't.

"I'm sorry, Gwen." Her fingertips slide from my neck as I step away, releasing her from my hold. A chill surrounds me.

She comes closer, but I hold my hand up.

Her mouth gapes, and hurt replaces her hunger. "You don't want me?"

"No." I curse myself when she recoils as if I slapped her. "I mean, I want you, but we can't...*I* can't do this."

"Why?" She crosses her arms.

"We barely know each other." I rub my hand over my jaw and sigh. "Gwen, you're still engaged."

Fire flares deep within her, and I take an involuntary step backward.

"As far as I'm concerned, my *fiancé* can go to the devil. I agreed to that farce of an engagement, but he wasn't *my* choice." Her voice softens. "I don't get a choice."

"Gwen...I..." Confusion spins in my brain. What does she mean? I reach for her, but she bats my hand away.

"I don't need your pity." She sniffs and keeps her distance, her eyes brimming with pain and shame. "I don't want it."

Shit. I didn't mean to upset her or dredge up her past or her current situation. I was trying to be a gentleman. It would have been easy to give in to the temptation and take her right there against the wall. But she deserves better than that...better than me.

"I'm so—"

"Stop." She holds up a hand. "I don't want to talk about it. Let's drop it, okay?"

"I just don't want to take advantage of you, Gwen." My soft declaration echoes through the quiet room.

Tears slip from her eyes, and guilt pierces my gut. I reach for her again, but she pulls away and retreats to the bedroom, closing the door behind her.

Fuck.

I flex my hand and force myself not to follow her. I didn't pull away from her kiss because I wanted to. I pulled away because I needed to. My chest pulls tight at the thought of leaving her in such a state, but I won't intrude where I'm not wanted.

It's hard not to take it personally. I hurt her, that's true, but it's more like I ripped open an old wound that hasn't healed properly and then poured alcohol on it. But I didn't inflict the original injury.

Not that it matters. Scars like that run deep.

For a few tense moments, I hope she'll come back. Pray she'll talk to me. Trust me. But I can't even trust myself when it comes to her. I would let her unleash hell on me if it would help her heal.

Even though she only walked into my life twenty-four hours ago, I feel like I've known her for years. Our connection is that strong. It leaves me wavering, questioning everything. One thing is certain, though. I won't use her for my own selfish pleasure or bind her to me with careless actions and thoughtless words. That's a line I won't cross.

I stare at the closed door and groan. There's nothing I can do tonight. Regret bites the back of my throat.

I haven't been drunk since I got back from Vietnam, and even though the thought of alcohol does nothing for me, my subconscious offers up the suggestion.

Instead of dwelling on my thoughts, I venture down to the bar. Jan, Dave, and Sam have things under control. It's not busy, but there's a small group in the far corner as well as a few regulars seated at the bar.

I grab a Coke and retreat to my office, closing the door behind me with my foot. There's a mountain of paperwork on my desk. I collapse in the chair and take a drink.

Her taste lingers on my tongue. Nothing will wash it away.

It's a memory I'll carry with me for years. I can't bring myself to regret it, but I won't allow myself to crave more.

Even as I try to convince myself it meant nothing, I palm myself through the fabric of my jeans. A quiet groan tears free at the pressure of my hand. I'm still hard, aching for her.

With a curse, I stand and lock the door. Resuming my seat, I take my cock out. It lays heavy in my hand. I close my eyes and grip it tight. It only takes a moment to imagine my large hand is her delicate one as I stroke myself.

Panting breaths fill the small space, and I relinquish myself to the fantasy. Gwen's bright eyes, her pouty lips, those dangerous curves. I want to bury my face between her thighs and not come up for air. I want her gasping my name, her fingers tangling in my hair as I lick her pussy. She'll moan, buck her hips against my mouth as I devour her. Right before she comes, I'll bury myself deep inside her.

My hand moves faster, stroking with a frantic purpose. The orgasm builds deep inside me. I squeeze my eyes closed and pump my fist, over and over. Visions of Gwen fill the darkness behind my lids. Her on her knees with her mouth wrapped around my length. Her beneath me as I bend her over the bar. Her straddling me in bed, hands braced on the wall as she rides my cock.

In my imagination, she tips her head back and cries out when she comes. It triggers my own release.

Warmth coats my hand as I come hard, my body shaking with the force of it. I can only imagine the reality would be more intense than my fantasy.

But it won't happen.

Somehow, despite my daze, I manage to clean myself with tissues and toss them into the trash. Mentally pushing aside the remains of my distraction, I pull the stack of papers close and open the top file.

I'll drown myself in paperwork if I have to, but there's no way I can go back upstairs. Not knowing she's in my bed. Knowing she wants me.

Whatever mess I've gotten myself into, I will find a way out of it. I always do.

I just hope I haven't fucked up beyond redemption.

Chapter Ten
Gwen

Heart racing, I collapse against the door.

Stupid. I lean my head back and pinch my eyes closed. How could I be so stupid?

I practically threw myself at Claude. What did I expect?

He's unlike any man I've ever met. Quiet, reserved…restrained.

My lips tingle with the memory of his kiss. Beneath his calm exterior beats the heart of a passionate man. I'd bet my life on it.

And yet…he turned me down. Pushed me away.

Am I that horrid for wanting something new, something real?

The floor creaks on the other side of the wall, and I hold my breath. A door closes in the distance, and I sag against the wood, alone and unwanted.

I curse myself as I head for the bathroom. When I catch a glimpse of myself in the mirror, I wince. I can't even face my own reflection after that fiasco. Turning my back to the sink, I brush my teeth with the new toothbrush Claude set aside for me.

He's thoughtful and kind. I shouldn't have pushed myself on him. I've made everything uncomfortable and awkward.

And yet…he leaned into my touch. His hard body pressed against mine. The undeniable ridge of his erection brushed my stomach. He wants me. There's no denying it. But his rigid sense of honor won't allow him to take what I offer. To embrace the heat between us.

I strip down and put on the pajamas he lent me before flopping onto his bed. His scent surrounds me. Nestling into the blankets, I inhale deeply, committing his aroma to memory.

My body squirms at the reminder of his presence, his touch,

his kiss. I huff and shift beneath the blankets. The soft glow of the bedside lamp flickers out when I press the switch.

Enshrouded in darkness, I stare at the ceiling. Nothing can purge Claude from my mind. He consumes my thoughts.

I slide my hand beneath the waistband of my shorts to find my pussy dripping for him. Those stolen moments of pleasure have left me in a state of need. I want him. All of him, not just the kind bartender who came to my rescue, the knight in shining armor. Even with his frustrating honor and chivalry, he has demons like any other man. Like me. There's more to Claude than he shows, and I want to peel his layers back, explore the darkness beneath.

My breath quickens as I imagine him stripping the clothes from my body, kissing his way down my bare skin. His head buried between my thighs. His soulful eyes locked with mine as he licks my pussy.

The fantasy pulls me deeper, and I circle my clit with two fingers. It's not enough.

I want to be filled by him. I want him to fuck all thought from my mind. To drive me to distraction before he makes me come, over and over, leaving me sated and suspended in bliss.

He'd tangle his hand in my hair while he drives deep from behind. Controlling me. Claiming me.

The men I've been with in the past, including Nick, cared nothing of my needs. For my pleasure. But I'm willing to bet Claude would make it his mission to satisfy me in ways I've only dreamed of. I imagine him pushing me to the edge and teasing me until I combust.

With every thought, the pleasure spirals higher until I'm positive I'll burst. The moment I picture him wrapping his hand around my throat, I come. Hard. Fast.

The orgasm radiates through me, and I milk it with gentle touches, arching my hips into my hand. As the effects wane, I roll to my side and sigh. It wasn't what I wanted, but it took the edge off. I still ache for him.

When I fall asleep, Claude greets me in my dreams. But even there, he plays the gentleman, and I drown in sexual frustration.

I wake to sunshine streaming through the window and the sound of movement in the next room. Peeling myself from the bed, I tiptoe to the door and peek into the living room.

"Good, you're awake." Quinn beams at me from the kitchen, her auburn curls woven into a braid over her shoulder. She pushes something in a skillet on the stove.

I open the door fully, and my gaze falls to the empty couch. "Where's Claude?"

"Down at the bar, most likely." She smiles and shakes her head. "I told you, he's married to that place."

"Are you making breakfast?" I cross the room and peer into the skillet.

"Yeah, figured you could use some girl time." Quinn points to a box on the floor behind the sofa. "I brought you some more clothes and other things you might need."

"Thanks." I fidget with the hem of the oversized shirt I'm wearing.

"Why don't you go get dressed and we can chat over breakfast?"

I carry the box into the bedroom. Inside is a variety of clothes, some makeup, hair products, deodorant, and a comfortable-looking pair of sneakers.

After I put on some clean underwear and a bra, I pull random articles from the box and match them the best I can. The stonewashed jeans and faded-black long-sleeved top are a definite step down from Gucci, but I'm not complaining. They're clean and comfortable. I'm grateful Quinn brought me something from her closet. While I enjoy Claude's oversized clothes, the lingering scent of him drives me crazy.

I wrangle my hair into a lopsided ponytail and brush on a little mascara. It's nothing fancy, but it does the trick.

When I return to the kitchen, Quinn is setting the second plate on the table.

She whistles low and winks. "You look smoking hot. Claude will love it."

My face heats at her praise. I'm used to compliments, but in my experience, they're nearly always insincere. Studying Quinn's face, I don't detect anything but honesty. I sit at the table across from her.

"How long have you known Claude?" I ask, pushing the eggs around on my plate.

"A few months," she says between bites. "We spend quite a bit of time together, now that I work in the bar four nights a week."

"You work at the bar?"

"Sure do." Quinn beams. "Grant isn't a fan of it, but he knows Claude won't tolerate anyone harassing his employees."

"Do you like it?"

"It's an honest living." She chews thoughtfully for a moment before setting aside her fork. "I was a thief when Grant met me. It's a long story."

I lean forward, curious. "I'd love to hear it."

"Of course, but not today. Claude told me he needs both of us downstairs by noon to get the bar ready."

"Ready for what?"

"Your first day." Quinn sips her coffee. "He asked me to keep an eye on you. Help you learn the ropes."

My face heats again. "I'm a fast learner. I promise."

"I don't doubt it." She narrows her eyes. "You look familiar. What did you say your last name was?"

"I didn't." I take a bite to hide my unease. I can't tell them my name. Not yet.

"Gwen." She reaches across the table to take my hand. "I promise, whatever happened to you, you're safe here."

"I know." With a sigh, I meet her gaze. "It's just...I like this. Being myself. Just Gwen. No expectations. No attachments."

"I understand." She squeezes my hand before releasing it. "Just know you can come to me any time if you want to talk."

A weight lifts from my chest. "Thanks."

We fall into general conversation about food and music. It seems we both have an affinity for Foreigner and Madonna. I reveal my burning love for Aerosmith, and she agrees wholeheartedly.

After we clean up, we head down to the bar. She knocks on the door to the office and pops her head in. "We're here," Quinn says to Claude, who glances up from his stack of papers.

"Good. Start with the prep work. I'll be out in a little while." His gaze shifts to me, and the butterflies that consumed me last night take flight again. "Morning."

I wave and smile, unable to speak, afraid I'll stick my foot in my mouth.

Quinn leads me into the bar and turns on the lights. She drops a few quarters into the jukebox and makes some selections. I sway with the bold strains of Journey, enthusiastic at her taste in music. Quinn and I are definitely kindred souls.

Thirty minutes later, we're laughing and singing to the music as we finish prepping. When the song finishes, Quinn nudges me with her hip.

"So feel free to tell me to get lost if I'm prying, but I've got to know." Her eyes sparkle. "What's going on with you and Claude?"

"Nothing." I grab a rag and wipe the counter.

"Come on." She leans closer. "I saw the way he looked at you during dinner last night. That *wasn't* nothing."

Heat creeps up my neck and into my cheeks. I shrug, unsure how to answer her. I turn to her and see Claude standing in the archway leading into the kitchen. Inside my chest, my heart flutters like a hummingbird.

His kind expression is impassive, but there's a tightness around his mouth that wasn't there the night we met.

"Are you done?"

Quinn spins around at his question. "Yes. We're ready to go."

"Are you sure this is what you want to do?" he asks, his gaze fixed on me.

"Positive."

He nods. "If there's any trouble, let me know. I'll take care of it."

"Why would there be trouble?" Quinn's confused gaze shifts from Claude to me.

"It's a long story." I offer a halfhearted smile.

"Looks like we're gonna have to make time to exchange long stories."

"Yeah." I rinse out the rag and drape it over the sink, ignoring the indecision twisting in my gut.

Maybe this isn't a good idea.

Claude's comment has left me floundering. It's possible Nick will return, searching for me. But I can't stay hidden away, living off charity. I can take care of myself; all I need is a chance to prove it.

When I turn around, Claude is gone. Quinn is leaning against the bar, watching me.

"What?"

"Nothing." She raises her hands and smirks. "But there's something going on between you two. I know it."

I busy myself with the tray of fruit to my right, hiding my red cheeks from her view. She's not wrong. There *is* something going on with Claude and me. But I want more than I should, more than he's willing to give. Right now, it's too complicated, and until I figure out what's going on in his mind, I don't want to confuse Quinn or Grant with complex explanations.

Whatever this is—even if we explored it—may not last. I shake my head. I'm not going to think about it. Not now. I want to enjoy this stint of freedom, for as long as I can, until I can figure out how to make it permanent. But that may require me to completely break ties with the city.

The last thing I want to do is lead Claude on and leave him with a broken heart when an opportunity arises. I doubt he'd be willing to come with me. It's not like he'd walk away from this place for a girl he just met. That's crazy.

But falling for a bartender in Hell's Kitchen after only two days seems insane too.

As we work, my mind keeps drifting to the soft-spoken bartender whose kiss left me breathless and wanting. Whatever happened between us, he's determined to ignore it. I just want to enjoy the moment. Can there be any compromise?

I will break down the wall he's built. One way or another.

CHAPTER ELEVEN
CLAUDE

I'm beginning to regret my decision to let her stay with me.

A week has passed quickly, and I'm left with an ache in my spine from the ancient sofa springs. I *could* find somewhere else to sleep or find her a place to live, but the truth is, I like having her here, even if I've been avoiding her like the goddamn plague.

I can't trust myself to be a gentleman. Not after that kiss. The temptation is too great, and I'm not the kind of guy who takes advantage of a vulnerable woman. Not that she's completely vulnerable. She's dangerous. Ripe curves, sweet smile, kind heart. But she's also engaged. I don't take that shit lightly.

I've done everything in my power to avoid her this week. I give her space. Hell, I've been showering and retreating to my office before she wakes every morning. I've done more paperwork this week than in the last six months.

Why is this so damned complicated? And who is Gwen really?

After a brief conversation with Grant, I make a few phone calls to see if anyone is looking for someone matching her description. There are plenty of missing women in the area, but apparently, none of them look like Gwen. No one can tell me anything.

I have nothing to go on but the name she gave me...and her nickname, Gigi. Both of these could be pseudonyms. I kick myself for not asking more questions the night her fiancé barged into my bar demanding information. I don't regret not giving her up that night. On the contrary, I'm glad the asshole left empty-handed.

That doesn't make her mine. It just makes this whole

situation fucking complicated. I should have never offered her a job or my bed.

Regardless, Gwen has shown she really is a quick learner. Even with no experience and no discernible skills, she works hard and takes no shit. In one week, she's not only learned how to do her job well, but she's become familiar with the regulars, who welcomed her as one of their own. I'm awestruck by the way she so seamlessly fits in. Who would have thought a debutante would be at home among blue-collar dockhands?

I push aside the last order request, then stand and stretch. A glance at the clock reminds me of my duties. Sam has to leave early tonight, and I promised to work the bar for him. The nights I stepped behind the bar this week put me in close proximity to Gwen, but the chaotic atmosphere kept us both busy. It took the restraint of a saint to not brush against her or whisper something to her in passing.

I wanted to. Lord knows I did.

Quinn took her to the corner thrift shop, and they came home, giggling, with six bags of clothes between them. She's blossomed from a wilting rose into a flower I don't recognize. Part of me wants to hide her, protect her. Someone with that much glow is bound to attract attention.

The bar is humming. Music blares from the jukebox, and nearly every table is full. A good night, so long as no trouble starts.

Quinn works the floor while Gwen mans the bar. I watch from the doorway for a moment as she pours pints and makes a dirty martini. She doesn't even reach for the cards to verify the recipe. Every pour is on point, and she makes it without error.

"Hey, Claude!" Frank, one of my regulars, shouts from his seat at the bar. A few of the patrons perk up at the sound of my name. I wave and step into the light.

Gwen turns, and her lips part in surprise before transforming into a smile when I cross the narrow space.

"I thought you were gonna leave me here all alone." She nudges me with her elbow.

"You were doing just fine all alone." I ignore the spark of

playfulness in her eyes…and the ache it causes in my chest.

"There you are." A woman's voice rises over the noise of the crowded bar. "Claude! Over here."

I scan the room until I spy a quartet of familiar faces at the end of the bar and smile. Rob and Arthur have brought their significant others here for their monthly double date.

"This place is packed tonight. What's the special event?" Rob asks, sidling up the bar with Marcy. Behind them, Arthur and his wife Kate look for open seats.

"No event. People just like to come here to blow off steam." I lean forward, resting my elbow on the bar.

"Guess the best-kept secret in New York is no longer a secret," Rob says with a smirk.

"You'll always have a table here if you bring these lovely ladies." I wink at Marcy, who grins in response. "What can I get for you?"

"The usual." Marcy nudges Rob aside. "We'll be in the booth at the back."

"I'll have Quinn bring your drinks."

Kate and Arthur wave before disappearing to a back booth where a group has just left. I shake my head and smile, watching Rob and Marcy join them. I've known Rob and Arthur for over a decade. Years ago, they saved my brother's life…and his job. I owe them both, but they treat me like family. I guess we are family in a way.

In the last few months, I've seen sides of them I never thought I'd see. Relaxed, carefree, and absolutely smitten. Of all the men in New York, I never thought *those* two would find happiness in relationships. As both were confirmed bachelors, it left me speechless when I met Kate and Marcy. But love shakes things up.

"What do you need?"

I turn to find Gwen standing beside me. Her soft floral perfume encircles her like a halo, driving away the scent of cigarettes and booze. Those blue eyes hold mine, and for a moment, I forget what she asked.

Drinks. Right.

"Can you make an old-fashioned and a martini with lemon?"

"No problem, boss." Gwen pivots and retrieves the ingredients.

I manage to shake myself free of her spell and make Rob's gin and tonic. What the hell am I doing? I can't keep going like this, with this tension simmering between us. We need to talk, but it's not going to happen until after closing. And even then, I'm tempting fate, because being alone with Gwen is damned torment.

I place two drinks on a tray, and Gwen appears with the other two drinks. Quinn arrives with an empty tray and gives me another order. I slide the full tray to her and motion to Rob and Arthur's table, where Grant has joined them. Of course he has.

Quinn sweeps the tray into her arms and sashays toward the table.

As Gwen works beside me, I'm hyperaware of her presence. We move in sync, brushing past each other, working in tandem. It's almost a dance. The teasing sway of her body as she moves, as she glides from one side of the bar to the other. Her hair grazes my arm when she spins around to use the register.

Fuck me. I don't know how much more of this I can take.

"Claude!"

I turn to Marcy, who's leaning on the bar. The crowd is thinning. It's after eleven, and there are open seats everywhere.

"What do you need, Marcy?"

"I was able to salvage that dress." She grins. "Took some work, but I got it clean. I'll bring it over next week."

"What dress?" Gwen's arm brushes mine as she joins the conversation.

"The Gucci one," I say. "Marcy's a stylist, and she offered to try to clean it."

"It's yours?" Marcy's brows nearly disappear into her tufted bangs. "Honey, I don't know what happened, but you need to take care with a dress of that caliber."

"Thank you so much." Gwen presses her hand to her chest. "It was a gift. I thought it was ruined beyond salvation."

"Luckily, I'm a master at removing bloodstains."

I purse my lips, biting back the question burning in my mind: how does one acquire that mastery? But I really don't want the answer.

"I owe you." She extends her open hand, and Marcy takes it. "I'm Gwen."

"Marcy." Her eyes narrow in thought as they shake hands. "Have we met? I have this crazy feeling I've seen you before."

"Oh, maybe. I've lived in the city my whole life. It's possible we've passed on the street."

"No…" Marcy rubs her jaw. "I swear you look familiar."

"I just have one of those faces, I guess." Gwen blushes and hedges, busying herself with wiping a dry spot on the cooler near her hip.

"Holy shit." Marcy's eyes fly wide. "That's it. You're Gigi Monroe."

Gwen's cheeks turn bright red, and she shushes Marcy. "Not so loud."

"Shit. Sorry." Marcy drops her voice. "What the hell are you doing working here?"

"I'll try not to take offense at that." I cross my arms, confused by the exchange and Marcy's revelation.

"That's not what I meant." She shoots me a look. "I'm just wondering why the daughter of the richest man in New York City is working as a bartender in Hell's Kitchen when she should be schmoozing with the in-crowd."

"It's a long story." Gwen sighs.

"Are you ready to go?" Rob comes alongside Marcy and kisses her cheek.

"Yeah." She takes a napkin and asks for a pen. I hand it to her and watch her scribble something down before giving it to Gwen. "For if you ever need a stylist. I also make custom designs on the side."

"Thanks." Gwen tucks it into her pocket and turns away from me.

After they've gone, she keeps her distance. Now I know why she's hiding. Why she's trying to start over.

She's a Monroe.

The sole heir to the wealthiest family in New York City. The goddamn cream of the elite.

A family notoriously close to the mafia.

Son of a bitch.

I take a long look at the handful of patrons in the bar. The moment they leave, this game comes to an end. Gwen will come clean.

Or I'll call her father and tell him to come pick up his daughter before she can completely, irrevocably shatter my heart.

CHAPTER TWELVE
GWEN

I saw the recognition light his eyes the moment Marcy's statement registered. Shit. There's no way I can play this off. He knows who I am, who my parents are.

Claude doesn't want me hanging around his bar. He doesn't want trouble. And that's all I am. Trouble in glitter and italics lit with neon light.

When he walks away without saying a word, I try not to take it personally. The unspoken tension between us has pulled tight over the past week. Even though he avoids me at every turn, it hums like an electrical current.

Instead of chasing after him, I busy myself behind the bar. There's still an hour until close. Quinn cleans the vacated tables while I focus on washing glasses.

Claude stands at the opposite end of the bar, talking with Tom, one of the regulars. It's difficult to ignore his presence. My attention gravitates to him as I work. His low voice drifts just under the music, making it impossible to hear what he's saying.

Quinn appears with a tray of dirty glasses. "There's only one table left and Tom. Should be able to clean up before closing tonight."

I nod and continue washing.

"Something wrong, hon?"

"I fucked up."

"How?"

There's no easy way to explain it, so I skip the details and go straight to the heart of my frustration. "Claude's upset with me."

Quinn scoffs. "Claude? No way. He's the most understanding man I know."

I shoot a glance in his direction. He remains firmly entrenched in his conversation with Tom. When I turn back to Quinn, her eyes are soft green pools of sympathy.

"Just talk to him. You'll feel better, I promise."

Before I can respond, Quinn turns and weaves through the tables. I stare at the far wall, my mind spinning with a hundred possible outcomes of a heart-to-heart with Claude, none of them ending well. I refocus on cleaning, and before I know it, the bar is empty.

Quinn locks the door at midnight. "Where's Claude?"

I scan the bar, but there's no sign of Claude or Grant. With a shrug, I place a few coins on the counter. "Put on some tunes while we work."

Quinn vacuums the floor while I mop behind the bar. We make quick work of the closing checklist, and for a brief moment, I forget my earlier concerns . To be honest, the music helps.

"I'll take the garbage out. Need anything else?" Quinn calls from the doorway.

"Nope, I can handle it from here. Go find your man." I wink.

She blows me a kiss and disappears into the kitchen.

Alone with my mop, I take my time, making sure to get under the shelves. A song by the Cars plays on the jukebox, and I sing along…of course I know the lyrics to "Magic." My body sways, and I'm caught up in the moment. The dim overhead lights reflect in the clean, wet floor.

My muscles ache nearly as much as my feet. I'm exhausted and sticky from some liquor I spilled on myself earlier, but there's nowhere I'd rather be. No upscale club or fancy dinner compares to the feeling of a job well done. Pride fills me, even as sadness tugs at the edges.

"It looks good." Claude's voice reverberates through me like a bell ringing in the darkness.

"Thanks." My face warms as I turn to face him.

He's leaning against the doorway, watching me, his brow furrowed.

"Something wrong?"

He presses his lips together and shakes his head.

I can't help but wonder if there's any way to cheer him up. Suddenly, I'm determined to make him smile, as if my life depended on it. "This is the second time you've caught me dancing." I set the broom aside. "Maybe you should join me."

"What?" His expression softens.

"Dance with me." I hold out my hand.

He straightens, but he doesn't move. "Gwen, I don't think that's a good idea."

"It's just a dance. I promise." I shimmy closer, moving my hips with each step. His breath hitches when I take his hand and pull him behind the bar. It's narrow, but I can dance anywhere.

He steps closer, and the music ends.

"I won't bite." I place his hand on my hip. Another song starts, "Cry to Me." It's bluesy and sexy.

I'm not sure I can keep my promise. I wrap my arms around his neck, and my body presses lightly against his as we sway.

His heavy sigh surrounds me, and I relax as his hand rests on my waist.

The memory of our kiss slams into me, but I bite my lip, stifling the urge to claim another one.

The music consumes me, and I grind against him. My hands wander over his shoulders, coming to rest on his chest.

He grabs my wrist and jerks me against him, pinning me against the bar.

"What do you want from me, Gwen?" Claude's deep voice is hoarse.

"The same thing you want." I trace my finger across his lips, trailing it over his broad chest. "I saw how much you wanted me when I was a scrappy, blood-covered wreck hiding in your bar."

"That's a bold assumption."

I shrug and lose myself in his whiskey-brown eyes, desperate to find some connection. Some revelation of truth. Of acceptance. "You want me, Claude. I can see it."

"You belong to someone else."

"No. I don't."

His eyes close for a breath, and when he opens them, I see hesitation amidst the pain. "You could have any man in the world. Why me?"

"You saw I needed help and stepped in." I lean into him, relaxing into his hold. I feel safe with him. Protected. Loved. "You didn't know anything about me. Not my name, not my family, nothing. You saw *me*."

Claude groans when I cup his cheek in my palm.

"You can't want this, Gwen. I'm no one."

"That may be true to the world." I bite my lip. "But not to me. You're *everything* to me."

"You don't know me."

"Then let me in."

"I can't." He hangs his head, and his voice cracks. "I'm broken and old. You don't want me."

"I do. You're kind." My fingers tip his chin up until our gazes lock. "And distinguished."

"I can't even hold you the way you should be held." He holds up his arms, making a show of his missing hand.

Without looking away, I rest my hand on the fabric covering where his hand should be. "You think that matters to me?"

"Doesn't it?"

"Not in the slightest." I slide my hand up his left arm, and he releases his hold on my other wrist. "I've seen you work. Nothing stops you from something when you set your mind to it. The only thing stopping us is *you*."

"Your fiancé, Gwen. What about him?"

I wince at the mention of Nick, but I shake off the nasty reminder and focus on the man in my arms. "I didn't choose him. I don't want him."

"It's not that easy."

"It is." I run my hand down the buttons of his shirt and over his belt buckle. My fingertips brush his cock, straining against the zipper of his pants. I grin at his sharp inhale. "The only man I want is standing right in front of me."

Claude dips his head and captures my lips in a bruising kiss. I cling to him, pulling him closer. The memories did no justice to the feel of him against me. Kissing me. His tongue delves into my mouth, and I moan at the onslaught of need. I'm a feather caught on the breeze, drifting higher and higher into the endless sky.

My hips rock against his thigh as his hand roams over my back, then caresses my ass. One massive palm grips me tight.

I want more.

His mouth trails across my jaw, my neck.

"Claude, please." I gasp against his shoulder as he runs his fingers along the crease where my thigh meets my ass. He grips my waist and spins me around, so my back is to his chest. I can see us in the mirror behind the bar. My tousled hair, flushed cheeks, kiss-swollen lips tell the same story as my lust-hazed eyes. I'm gone, lost in him.

"Hands on the counter." His brash command has my pussy weeping.

I place my hands on the sturdy counter beneath the shelves. His talented fingers unfasten my jeans and slide them down my hips. The cool air bites my thighs as he settles the denim at my ankles.

His fingers trail over the inside of my thighs as he slowly rises. In the mirror, I watch his dark head as he arches into me, blocking me with his body. His heat steadies me. When his palm cups my pussy through the thin fabric of my panties, I whimper.

"You don't have to be quiet for me, sweetheart." He pushes aside the fabric and glides his long fingers across my slick folds, parting them. "Is this what you want?"

"Yes. God, yes," I cry out when he slides a finger into me, stroking my sensitive walls. "Claude," I gasp as he adds another finger and slowly fucks me.

When I meet his gaze in the mirror, he smiles, and it's everything I ever dreamed of. His smile ignites something visceral inside of me. I rock against his hand, needing pressure against my clit. Claude quickens his pace, grinding the heel of his palm against my pelvis. Sweet tension spirals higher and higher. I tremble and shake as he moves deeper, pivoting his thumb to find my clit swollen.

"Come for me, sweetheart," he whispers in my ear, adding a little more pressure.

I buck my hips into his hand, and my climax slams into me. When I come, his name is on my lips followed by a string of curses.

I've never come that hard. Ever.

Claude kisses my shoulder, and I lift my head to meet his gaze. He spins me around, and my arms go around his waist. This time his kiss is tender.

"Shall we go upstairs?" I mutter against his mouth.

"Fuck, yes, that sofa will kill me if I spend one more night on it."

"You were always welcome to join me." I kiss him again, savoring the taste of him. "That bed is too big for one person."

"You'll be the death of me." He grins. "But what a fucking way to go."

I shimmy back into my jeans and follow Claude upstairs.

Finally. Fucking finally.

Chapter Thirteen
Claude

What the fuck am I doing? I'm too far gone to care.

She follows me. I pause at the base of the stairs and allow her to go first. Her ass sways with each step, and I'm mesmerized by it. I can't wait to get those clothes off, to see all of her.

Her coming apart in my arms, moaning my name as her climax grips my fingers…it's the sexiest thing I've ever experienced.

I've been with women…before I lost my hand and part of my arm, before I sacrificed at the request of my country. When I came home, people looked at me differently. Treated me differently. They never thanked me for my service or my sacrifice. I didn't expect it.

But I never expected to feel like an outcast in my own neighborhood, among the people I grew up with either.

Years of working in the bar gave me purpose, a way to remind society I wasn't worthless, even with my injury. But when it came to women, I was still an outcast. Shunned for my quiet nature and lack of two functional hands.

Gwen opens the door to my apartment. She spins to face me when I close it. Her blue eyes sparkle in the low lamplight as she takes hold of my button-down shirt.

"I'm all sticky. From work," she says, grinning. She slowly slips the buttons free, her lashes fluttering against her cheeks as she makes quick work of my shirt. "I should shower."

"Don't let me stop you." I wrap my hand around the back of her neck, and she leans into the touch.

"Join me." Her hand trails up my stomach and rests on my heart.

Fuck, her touch has me hard as a granite boulder, as if I wasn't hard enough already.

"There's room for two."

"I doubt that." There's really not enough room for *me* in my shower, but she's insistent.

"We'll make room." She steps back, eyeing my chest and licking her lips. As she turns, heading for the bedroom, she peels the shirt from her torso and drops it to the floor.

I sway at the sight of her bare spine. Fuck. She wasn't wearing a bra this whole time. How did I not notice?

Then I remember how desperate I was to avoid her…to avoid this.

I was an idiot. She pauses in the doorway and glances at me, her body pivoting enough to show the generous curve of her breast and a soft, peaked nipple.

"Are you coming?"

"Not yet, but I'm close," I mutter under my breath even as my feet take action.

Gwen heads for the bathroom, shedding more clothing along the way.

I pull my shirt off, tossing it aside as I follow her. I fumble with my pants, unable to grip the button.

"Let me help." Gwen takes the button in her hands and unfastens it. As she slides the zipper down, her gaze dips to my waist. She hooks her thumbs into my jeans and pulls them down, taking my underwear with them. On her knees, she grasps my cock in her hands.

I brace my hand on the wall when she takes me in her mouth.

I nearly lose control at the sight of her full lips stretched around me. Her pink cheeks glow as she hums, the sound vibrating through my flesh.

"Fuck, Gwen." I gasp as she cups my balls and takes me deeper. As she pulls back, her tongue swirls around the head, and I nearly come. "Baby, if you keep going, I won't be able to stop."

She wipes her mouth with her thumb before rising to her feet. Every curve is bare, and I'm struck stupid at the sight of the woman before me. How the hell did I get so lucky? I can't even think about it. If I think too much, I might wake up and realize this is all a dream.

But it's not.

With a wink, Gwen disappears into the bathroom.

I kick off my shoes and pants before stumbling into the bathroom after her, my cock leading the way.

She bends over to turn on the shower, and the sight of her ass, with her soft folds bared to me, unleashes a beast. I hook my arm around her waist and pull her back against me. My cock rubs against her slick center, and she moans.

With the water running, the small space slowly fills with steam. My hand delves between her thighs to stroke her clit.

"Claude, please."

Her breathy plea tips me over the edge. I angle my hips and press the tip of my cock against her warm entrance. She reaches down to guide me in.

Holy shit.

She grips me tight as I drive deep into her. Her guttural moan echoes off the tiles.

It's been a while, but I never remember it feeling this fucking good. Like coming home, like being welcomed with open arms. I must have died and gone to heaven.

Being inside her leaves me breathless and panting. I hold tight as she bucks against me, taking me even deeper.

My balls ache. If she keeps this up, I'm going to come. I'll fill her until her pussy weeps with my cum.

The thought makes me feral. Possessive. I want to mark her, to ruin her with pleasure.

"Mine," I growl, withdrawing and thrusting into her, over and over.

"Yours," she agrees, whimpering, arching into the movements, taking me without hesitation.

Her fingers replace mine on her clit, and I band my arm around her chest, placing my hand on her throat. Her back bows, but she's pliant and willing in my arms.

The steam clouds my vision, but I don't need to see. I *feel* everything. Gwen melts into me. Her moans and panting breaths echo off the walls.

Gwen is mine. I am hers. Bound together like this, I've never been more grounded, more certain of anything in my entire life.

Her breaths quicken as she rubs her clit in tempo with my thrusts. I double my efforts, praying I hold out until she comes. I'm close. Too close. I'm amazed I've lasted this long. Her pussy grips me tighter.

"Come for me again, sweetheart," I murmur against her ear. "I want it."

She pushes her ass back, urging me on, wanting more. I oblige with a tilt of my hips.

Deeper. Harder. More.

I grit my teeth as her pussy tightens around my cock. Her orgasm ripples through her, and she cries out.

My body relinquishes control. I come hard, filling her.

Gwen collapses against me, and I hold her there. Our breaths mingling with the steam, our hearts racing in tandem.

I'm so fucking obsessed with this woman. I can't get enough. Even though I've just come, my cock is still hard inside her.

I press a kiss to her cheek and slide free. My cum leaks down her thigh and pride fills me. I should be ashamed because I wasn't careful. She could get pregnant, and whatever this is will become more complicated. But a secret part of me wants her to carry our child.

What the hell am I even thinking?

"I'm sorry." I drop my hand, letting it glide down her arm until it's by my side.

She turns and wraps her arms around my neck. "For what?"

"Not using protection."

"I'm on the pill." She rises up on her toes and kisses my lips.

I'm drunk on her touch.

"Still." My mind blanks when her hands glide down my arms, stopping to rest on my biceps.

"I liked it." A mischievous smirk plays on her mouth. "*Mine,*" she growls before kissing me again.

I blame the steam billowing around us for the heat in my face. "Take your shower."

Gwen takes my hand and guides me into the shower beside her. It's a tight fit, but I lean against the wall, and she steps into the spray. The sticky mess from work along with the remnants of our passionate sex swirl down the drain.

When she finishes washing herself, she takes the soapy washcloth and slides it over my chest. I'm more than capable of washing myself, but the way she moves the cloth across my skin leaves my heart aching, my mind blank, a blissful smile on my lips.

She cleans me with the same efficiency I've seen in the bar when she works. Dedicated, mindful, tender. She washes one arm, then the other, gentle when she reaches the stub where my forearm used to be.

"Do you miss it?" she asks, meeting my gaze before chuckling. "Of course you do. That's a stupid question. Sorry."

"Don't be sorry." I smile at her flustered expression. "It's been gone so long, I barely remember what it was like to have it."

"It hasn't stopped you."

"No."

"I'm glad." She lowers the rag and strokes my cock through the cloth.

I inhale sharply, sucking air through my teeth. Arousal spikes through me, and I need to be inside her again. Grasping her close, I switch our positions and rinse away the soap before turning off the shower.

"I'm not done." She pouts.

"Neither am I, sweetheart." I kiss her, arching my hips against her stomach.

She tangles her fingers in my wet hair and returns the kiss with unrestrained hunger. When we finally break apart, I wonder if we increased the steam in the room. Her blue eyes are dark, like midnight over the ocean.

She licks her lips. "Can I..."

She blushes, and I'm intrigued by her sudden shyness.

"Whatever you want, sweetheart."

Gwen squeals with joy and steps out of the shower, reaching for a towel. We both dry off, and I leave her in the bathroom while I move to the bed. She'll join me when she's ready.

Whatever she wants from me, I'm more than happy to give it to her.

She's mine as much as I'm hers. That thought alone makes me deliriously happy.

I'll savor every moment because God knows when it'll come to an end.

It always does.

CHAPTER FOURTEEN
GWEN

My body is humming. I knew beneath that calm exterior beat the heart of a passionate lover.

I quickly dry my body and my hair, braiding it over my shoulder. I stare at the woman in the mirror. The familiar face greets me, but gone are the dark circles beneath my eyes, replaced by a glow I've never seen before.

A smile steals across my lips. For the first time in my life, I'm happy. Content.

As much as I want Claude, I know I'm playing with fire. Can this last? I don't know. But now that I've had a taste, I'm going to damn well try to make it work.

The butterflies in my stomach take flight at the thought of him waiting for me in the bed. After two orgasms, I'm hungry for more. I've never been with a man who put my pleasure first, who took his time, who savored every kiss, every moan of pleasure.

Hearing him stake his claim while offering himself in return is the sexiest thing I've ever experienced.

Mine. Yours.

Damn. I'm wet and ready for him again.

Draping the towel over a hook behind the door, I catch one last glimpse of myself. Kiss-bruised lips. Eyes dark with need. Skin flushed from heat.

When I open the door, I'm unprepared for the sight awaiting me. Claude's naked, sitting on the bed, back against the headboard. His long legs are crossed at the ankles, his eyes closed. My gaze drops to his cock, stiff against his thigh.

He looks like a goddamn warrior waiting for his victor's reward.

I bite my lip. *All mine.*

"You tired already?"

"No." His eyes snap open and fix on me. "Just resting before round two."

"So confident."

My hips sway as I approach the bed. His gaze dips down the length of my body like he's committing every inch to memory.

"I like that in a man."

He scoffs but doesn't say anything.

I trail my fingertips along his thigh, climbing higher until they brush the tip of his cock.

He sucks in a breath. "Don't tease me, Gwen."

His dark gaze matches the tone of his voice. He's holding back, straining with desperate need.

I climb onto the bed and straddle his thighs, rubbing myself along his length. "Who says I'm teasing?"

His hand rests on my hip as I guide him inside me.

He's deep, filling me in a way he didn't before, touching parts of me that have nothing to do with sex.

I rock my hips, ride him slowly.

"Damn it, Gwen," he gasps, meeting my movements with gentle motions of his own.

"You like that?" I murmur and grip his shoulders. He's solid beneath my touch. His muscles flex with bridled restraint.

He nods and stifles a groan. "Sweetheart, you're killing me."

His words encourage me to move faster, drive him deeper, take all of him, body and soul. *Mine.* The confession lingers in my mind, spiking my desire.

My knees ache, but I push myself more. My arousal spirals higher with every thrust. I meet his gaze, lose myself, focus solely on him, chase the pleasure dancing just out of reach.

"That's it, baby. Take what you need." The pad of his thumb presses my clit, making me buck my hips.

"Oh, fuck." Sparks dance in my vision as the sensations spike.

How does he know exactly what I need?

The pressure increases as he makes urgent circles, sending

jolts of pleasure rocketing through my core.

His breath deepens, erratic between moans and muttered curses as my pussy clenches around him.

I'm deliriously close to coming, but my body refuses to relent.

"You gonna come for me, sweetheart?"

The question echoes around my brain. The switch flips when he gently pinches my clit and slides his fingers through my folds.

An orgasm rips through me, tearing a desperate moan from my throat. I dig my fingernails into his skin and hold tight, afraid I might float away if I let go. He fucks me through my climax, and when I drift down from my high, I feel him come, filling me, making me a sticky, sated mess once more.

He leans his forehead against mine. "Good girl."

I've never preened under someone's praise before, but his words unleash a glowing warmth within me. I collapse against his chest, and he wraps his arm around me. His heartbeat resonates with mine, falling into a calming rhythm.

After a few moments, he kisses my forehead. "We should get some rest."

With a disappointed groan, I roll off him and curl up on the bed. Claude stands and disappears into the bathroom.

I nestle in the warm spot he vacated and sigh. Sex has never left me so blissfully exhausted.

Claude reappears with a warm rag and wipes me clean. His kindness leaves me in a gooey puddle. I can't help but want this man, with his consideration and his heart of gold.

When he climbs back into bed, he lays on his back and gathers me against his chest. My head rests in the crook of his shoulder, my hand on his beating heart.

We're like two puzzle pieces who fit perfectly together.

The cool air soothes my heated skin. Even though it's the first week of December, I'm overheated, tucked against him. He's an inferno, but I bask in his radiance. Within moments, I drift to sleep, content and safe in his arms.

When I stir from a dreamless sleep, it's well past dawn, and sunlight filters through the thin curtains. I'm curled around Claude, my thigh thrown over his, my hand on his chest, moving with the steady rhythm of his deep slumbering breaths.

I steal a glance at his face. He's so handsome. Some would disagree, with his crooked nose and the constellation of moles crisscrossing his pale face. But his inner strength bleeds through, even when he sleeps. A soft smile lingers on his lips, barely noticeable. I want to kiss him, steal that smile for my own.

But a wicked, playful thought strikes me.

Gently sliding from his embrace, I tug down the blanket and wrap one hand around his cock. He moans and shifts, but doesn't wake. His cock, however, swells. I stroke him slowly, savoring the heavy weight in my hand. He's soft as velvet and thick. Precum leaks from the tip, and I lick it away.

Bold curiosity takes control. I've never been a fan of blow jobs, but I want to see Claude lose control. Eager, I take him deep into my mouth, until he touches the back of my throat.

"Oh, God." Claude arches his hips off the bed, pushing into my mouth.

I look up and find him staring at me, his eyes glazed with sleep and lust. He runs his hand through my hair.

I wrap my hand tighter around his base and fuck him with my mouth. He thickens against my tongue, and I bask in the control I have over his pleasure. My pace quickens, and his hold on my hair tightens.

He gasps and pants, moaning when I hit a particularly sensitive spot.

I repeat the motion, driving him higher and higher.

He tries to draw me away, but I tighten my grip. I want *all* of him.

"Goddamn, Gwen," he cries out when he comes.

I swallow every drop.

He grins, and I'm smitten with his carefree, orgasmic glow. I did that. Pride fills me at my ability to disarm him with only my mouth and the promise of pleasure.

But there's more beneath it. A lingering sense of peace. Like this is where I'm meant to be. With him, in this moment.

I never want to leave.

Claude pats his chest, inviting me back into his embrace. When I'm settled beside him, he wraps his arm around my shoulder and kisses me.

"Thank you," he whispers against my lips.

"For what?"

"I've never been woken up with a blow job." He grins. "A guy could get used to it."

Gooey warmth fills me at his words. I settle against him, resting my head on his chest.

We lay in silence for what seems like forever. He traces patterns across the back of my hand with a finger. I hold him tight, losing myself in the beautiful simplicity of this moment. No expectations. No demands. Just two people consumed by desire and a need for connection.

"Why did you choose my bar?" Claude's question shakes me from my thoughts.

"It was snowing hard. I needed to hide from…him. The glow of your sign was a beacon."

"Can I ask why you ran away from your fiancé?"

I pinch my eyes closed, the desire to trust Claude warring with the pain of reliving the horror of that night. I take a deep breath and search for the right words.

"I understand if you don't want to tell me." His hand stops caressing mine.

"He asked me to help him with a job."

"A job?" Claude furrows his brow.

"Yeah." I blow out a shaky breath. "He asked me to seduce someone."

Claude scowls, his eyes darkening. "Your fiancé asked you to seduce someone else? Why?"

"Blackmail, extortion, who knows?" Panic grips me at the reminder of his betrayal. I knew he wasn't a good man, but this request broke me. I couldn't follow through with my father's demand to marry him when I would have to sell my soul in the process. "When I said no, he grabbed me, threatened to carve his name into my skin, to remind everyone who I belonged to."

My voice trembles.

Claude sits up and gathers me to him. I cling to his torso, burying my face into his chest. He runs his hand up and down my arm, slowly pulling me from the memories back into the present.

"That's why you hurt him."

I nod. "When I hit him in the nose, it gave me a chance to get away. I ran through the snow until I reached your bar. It was a gamble, asking for help. But I had to try. I couldn't live life bound to a man who would brand me and demand I debase myself for his pleasure."

"Did you know he was like this?"

"Yes. He has a reputation for being cold and cruel. All the DeLucas are. He's the youngest son of the head of the family."

"Fuck." Claude tightens his hold on me.

"My father owes the mob a fortune." I bite my lip, terrified of the consequences if I voice everything I know. The details could get me killed...or worse. "He promised me to Nick DeLuca, a mutually beneficial arrangement."

Claude's breath hitches. "I'm so sorry, Gwen."

I snuggle closer, wanting to hide from the horrible reality of my past. For years, I felt like an outsider in my own family. A golden trinket, a pawn in my father's deals. A media darling to draw attention away from the family's questionable actions, from their dark, backroom negotiations. They foisted me into the spotlight, using me as a glittering, compliant distraction. And I let them. For years.

But no more.

When I'm with Claude, I realize what I've been missing all these years. Love and connection. Compassion and trust. Here, I'm safe and warm. Loved.

What we have might have come in with a snowstorm, but in the warmth of the sun, I know beyond anything, I can never go back to the life I once knew. Not when I know what true happiness feels like.

Being with Claude completes me in ways I never imagined possible. I may be a fool to throw away the glitz and glamour, but I'd sacrifice it all in a heartbeat if it means I can spend the rest of my life with Claude.

I can't say it aloud. It sounds insane. But I can show him. In every touch, every kiss, every glance. This may be the craziest thing I've ever done, but I don't care. I love him. I'd be even crazier to let him go.

I just hope he loves me too.

CHAPTER FIFTEEN
CLAUDE

The phone rings, shattering our tender moment of bliss. I was only a breath away from the confession of my life. Of course the phone interrupts.

With a kiss to her forehead, I roll off the bed and dart, naked, into the living room before the ringing stops.

"This had better be an emergency," I growl into the receiver, not caring who could possibly be on the other end.

"Am I interrupting something?" Grant's voice digs into my last remaining nerve and twists.

"Yes."

"Shit." Grant groans as the implication goes unspoken. "You're not gonna like this."

"What?"

"I called the station this morning to get an update from Mickey." He pauses, and it's almost like I'm waiting for a bullet to strike. "There was a missing person's report filed for Gwen last night. With a reward for any information to her whereabouts and safe return."

"Fuck." I keep my voice low, hoping it doesn't carry into the open bedroom door. A quick glance tells me she's in the bathroom. "What happens next?"

"That is entirely up to you, Claude."

Grant's words carry that older, wiser brother tone. I wince at the underlying truth within them.

"They won't stop until they find her." I sigh. "And if they find her with me, shit's gonna hit the fan."

"More than likely."

"I can't turn her in."

"Not saying you have to."

"You act like I have a choice." I watch the bedroom,

keeping an eye out for Gwen's return from the bathroom.

"You do."

"Goddamn it." I bite back the frustration, and it turns to acid in my throat. "Give me a day to think about it."

"Okay, but do yourself a favor and tell her they're looking for her." Grant sounds sympathetic, which is unexpected. "If she knows, she can decide for herself."

"Got it." I shift my weight when Gwen appears beyond the doorway, her skin glowing in the morning sunshine. "Thanks."

Without waiting for my brother's response, I hang up the phone.

Gwen leans against the doorframe. My gaze wanders slowly down her generous curves. Pained regret stabs me, even as my cock twitches in appreciation.

I can't do it. I can't tell her. I can't ruin this perfect moment of domestic bliss.

I've craved it for so long, thinking it was beyond my reach. But it's right here, standing in front of me. Better than Kodachrome.

"Something wrong?"

I stiffen at her question, and she notices before I can shake it off. Her mouth pulls into a frown.

"No," I lie. "That was Grant. He always leaves me in a sour mood when he calls this early."

Her smile returns. My heart breaks over the little white lie. I have to tell her, but it can wait.

Right now, I want what we had last night. This morning. I want it to bleed into the rest of the day. A taste of what we could have in a perfect world. Something. Anything but the shitty cards we were both dealt.

I want to keep her for myself, but she needs to know her family is looking for her. And they deserve to know she's alive and well.

I have two choices. Turn her in, or tell her and encourage her to do it herself. Deep down, I know she won't do it. She's made her stance perfectly clear. She has no desire to return to that life or to the man her parents want her to marry. It's a catch-

22, no matter how I figure it.

She steps into my embrace, wrapping her arms around my waist and resting her head against my chest. I want to keep her like this forever, but if I do and there's no closure with her family, it'll bite me in the ass.

"Are you hungry?" Her question breaks through my complicated thoughts.

"Starving." I kiss the top of her head. "Let me put on some pants, and I'll make breakfast."

"I'll help." Gwen bounds into the bedroom and puts on an old tee shirt. I admire the sight of her bare ass as she draws up a pair of dainty underwear, hiding it from view.

"Pancakes?" she asks, pausing in the doorway.

"And crispy bacon," I add with a smile.

"Crispy?" She scrunches her nose, and it takes every ounce of restraint not to pull her back into the room and bury myself between her thighs once more. "Not too crispy. If you burn it, it ruins the flavor."

I chuckle and shake my head. I'll never get enough of this woman. Ever. Even with her culinary misconceptions.

Her soft singing echoes through the apartment as she rummages in the refrigerator. I ignore her siren song and grab a pair of clean sweatpants from the dresser. Tugging on an old flannel shirt, I slowly button it with my one hand.

Gwen crosses the room to finish the job for me.

"I can do it myself."

"I know, but I wanted to help." Her eyes are like a crystalline ocean in a Caribbean vacation magazine. "Where's the mix?"

"Top shelf." I open the cabinet and pull down a box of Aunt Jemima's buttermilk pancake mix. When I hand it to her, she does a little dance. It seems a little over the top for pancakes.

She glances up and sees the expression on my face. "What? Our cook never made pancakes. Mom refused to serve them since she believed they were empty calories and made her fat." She pulls out a measuring cup and begins to scoop the mix into a bowl.

"So how do you know you like pancakes?" I steer the conversation away from her mother's controlling insecurity.

"Alfred, our chauffeur, used to sneak them to me when he drove me to school." Her eyes sparkle at the memory. "I was obsessed! Still am."

"I can tell." I turn on a burner and place a skillet on the stovetop. My unwavering moral compass demands I test the waters, and I carefully broach the subject burning a hole in my brain. "So you ran away because your mom refused to let you have pancakes?"

Her hand pauses midmix, and she spins to face me. For a moment, I wonder if I crossed a line, but when she sees my teasing smirk, she relaxes.

"No." She goes back to slowly stirring the batter, her eyes unfocused and dazed as she loses herself in thought.

I put a second pan on for the bacon and place some slices in it. She'll talk when she's ready. If I push, she'll clam up completely.

Her sigh twists the blade in my already bleeding conscience.

"My family is shit. They treat me worse than a servant. I'm nothing more than a pawn to them. There was no love in my childhood, only secrets and lies." Her words pour free, and even as she speaks them, I can feel their weight bearing down on her…and on me.

"They used me," she continues. "All the time. It's miserable. And their pristine image of wealth and success…it's a total sham. They're so wrapped up with the mob, it's only a matter of time until they're caught. They have to be. I mean, that's how it works, right?"

I study her closely. She's not really asking me, is she?

"We're always taught good guys win and bad guys go to jail." Gwen continues as she sets aside the batter and takes my hand. "That's how it works."

I pull her against me to hold her close. I can't tell her the truth, but I can't lie. "I wish it was, sweetheart. But this isn't a fairy tale. There's not always a happy ending."

She buries her face in my shirt. "I just want to stay here with you, forget they even exist."

That simple confession leaves me breathless with joy. "I would love that, Gwen."

"Really?" She draws back, eyes glistening with unshed tears.

"Really." I smooth her hair away from her face and kiss her forehead. "But they're not going to let you go easily."

"I know."

The sound of her breaking heart mirrors my own. If she only knew how much I want to ride in to save her, slay her dragons, give her the life she deserves. But it wouldn't solve the fundamental problem.

"The only way you'll have peace is if you break ties with them. Officially."

"If I go back"—her grip tightens—"they'll never let me go."

"You never know until you try."

Her eyes meet mine. The terror and uncertainty I find there ignites a fire of possessiveness I don't recognize.

Mine.

"I don't want to lose you," she says.

"You'll never lose me, sweetheart." I press a soft kiss to her lips. "I promise."

I know better than to make promises I can't keep, but desperation drives me beyond reason. All I want is to see her smile, to keep her safe.

How the hell am I supposed to go up against the richest man in Manhattan *and* the mafia to protect this woman I love?

Chapter Sixteen
Gwen

After a bliss-filled day with Claude, responsibility pulls us back to reality. By six o'clock, we're both behind the bar, slinging drinks to an eager, after-work crowd.

I could have bottled up my time with Claude and kept it in my pocket. A perfect memory to carry forever. But all good things must come to an end, even if temporarily.

Casting sly glances at him while I work leaves my face flushed and my heart fluttering. Deep inside the calm, relaxed bartender lies the soul of a romantic. His passion and dedication, once unleashed, know no bounds.

How can I *not* love him? I must be crazy for thinking this way.

I slide a beer across the bar to Tom and turn to find Claude smiling in my direction. I return it, wondering if he can read my thoughts.

If he could, he'd blush three shades of red before dragging me to the back office and bending me over the desk. I know it. The thought leaves my knees weak and my panties damp. I lick my lips and return to work. There'll be time enough for that later. Right now, I have thirsty patrons to serve.

Every table in the bar is full. There are a handful of unoccupied seats at the bar. It's already a busy night. That's good. It makes the shift go faster. Even though I enjoy the job, I can't wait to lock the doors and take Claude upstairs.

"Can you take this to table five?" Claude places a few drinks on a tray and gestures to the other side of the room.

"Got it." I take the tray, careful not to spill anything.

"Good girl," he whispers against my ear.

My body hums with need, and I'm even wetter than before. Why would he say that to me in public? I bite back a whimper and glare at him. His smirk tells me he knows *exactly* what those two words did to me.

I brush past him, confidently carrying the tray with one hand. Weaving through the crowd proves a little tricky, but I make it without incident. With a smile, I dole out the drinks and ask if they need anything else.

The door opens and a gust of cold air breezes through the warm room.

I glance up, and my blood turns to ice in my veins.

Nick and two cronies stand at the entrance. They scan the crowd, searching for someone. For me.

Shit. He's back. I knew he would return, but I didn't think it would be so soon. I hoped to be long gone before it happened. That was before Claude and I—

Nick's gaze settles on me, and a thin, wicked smile curves his mouth. His nose is red and there's a bandage across the bridge, but he's still drawing attention. Most would call him handsome with his bright blue eyes, his thick black hair, and his custom suit. But he's a wolf in sheep's clothing. His looks, his charms…they're an act. A damn good act, but still bullshit. He's dangerous. I've heard him brag about the vile shit he's done. And when he tried to pull me into his twisted world, I drew the line.

My spine straightens as he approaches. I should run, but he'll chase me. It's no use. I don't want to cause a scene or for anyone to get hurt. Especially Claude.

"There you are, baby." He wraps his arm around my shoulders. "I was so worried about you."

I cringe at the overpowering scent of his cologne. *Obsession.* I'll never be able to smell it without immediately thinking of Nick. He pulls me closer to him, and I gag.

"What the hell do you want?" I snarl, fighting the nausea.

"Is that any way to talk to your fiancé?" He leads me toward the two goons standing near the door. "Your parents were worried. They offered a reward for your safe return."

"A reward?"

My gaze darts through the crowd and lands on Claude, watching from behind the bar, his eyes narrowed, his fist clenched around a towel. I want to call to him. Run to him. But I can't. Nick has me pinned to his side.

If I fight him, he'll hurt me. And if he does that, Claude will try to save me. Nick won't hesitate to shoot him. The gun he carries in a holster beneath his jacket digs into my shoulder. This could become a bloodbath if I fight. Instead, I keep him talking, distracted.

"Yeah." His laugh makes my skin crawl. "I should've known the bartender squirreled you away during that storm. Bet you fucked him in exchange for a job, didn't you?" His breath burns my neck as he murmurs his caustic words. "Whore."

I swallow the bile stinging my throat. "Please don't hurt him."

"Was it worth it?" he asks, his voice low.

I bite my lip. He's baiting me, trying to draw me into a reaction. As soon as he gets me alone, he'll unleash on me, so I keep my mouth clenched shut. I refuse to give him any ammunition against me. Or against Claude.

"How did you know I was here?" I breathe deeply, concentrating on not jerking away from his touch.

"Got a tip." He grins and turns his attention to Claude, whose countenance mirrors a thundercloud over a midnight sea. "Give him the reward." He nudges one of the goons and steps back. "I'm taking her home."

What? Disbelief fills me. My gaze flashes from Nick's self-satisfied smirk to Claude, leaning against the bar, watching us intently.

Tears fill my eyes. Did he call my parents? Tell them where I was? No. That can't be.

Panic chokes me. Claude's whiskey-brown eyes don't waver, even as Nick drags me to the door. He ignores the goon closing the distance between us. I shake my head, and he crumbles, finally dropping his gaze.

Nick opens the door and drags me into the cold December air. Goosebumps prickle my arms, and I shiver at the drastic shift in temperature. My legs shake, my heart wrenches in two.

Claude sold me out. I choke back a sob as the realization

takes root in my soul.

Nick opens the car door and shoves me into a waiting Rolls Royce. I curl into a ball on the leather seat, keeping my distance from him as he slides in beside me.

The two goons get in the front, and the engine roars to life. Warmth fills the car's interior, but I can't stop trembling. After a few minutes, the cold wears off, but I'm still shaking. From fear. From rage. From disbelief. From pure heartbreak. From all of it.

"Did you enjoy your week of slumming, Gigi?" Nick asks, lighting a cigar. Smoke fills the car, making me cough.

I turn to watch the street outside, keeping quiet.

"Would you rather I torch the place? Burn the old heap to the ground?" He chuckles. "Might be an improvement."

I bite my tongue. He's doing it on purpose. Ignore him.

"I could buy the dump, turn it into my personal playground." He grips my chin and turns me to face him. "I'd fuck you on that bar in front of everyone. Then they'd know exactly who you belong to."

My jaw clenches. The image he paints leaves my stomach sour. I push his hand away. "I'd rather die than let you touch me."

"Is that so?" His dark eyes sparkle in the passing light from outside the car. "Too bad I have an agreement with your father. That contract is legally binding." He bares his teeth in an evil grin. "If you don't hold up your end of the deal, your whole family will pay the price, you selfish bitch."

"Go to hell."

"Been there, baby, and they love me." He leans back and runs his hand over his bulging cock. "Why don't you come over here, show me how much you missed me?"

"I'd rather die."

He grips the back of my head and drags me into his lap. "Your little adventure has made you a smart-mouthed cunt."

"Fuck you, Nick." I hold his gaze. "Unless you want another broken nose, I suggest you let me go."

His grip tightens on my neck, and I flinch.

"You got lucky." His voice is low, deceptively calm.

My blood runs cold.

"Once you're my wife, I'll make sure you know your place. If you cross me again, I will fucking kill you."

His threat pierces my soul. I swallow the lump in my throat as terror sinks into my bones. He means it.

When he releases me, I slink back to my side of the car and hug my knees to my chest. I should have run. Left the city. Burned every bridge behind me. Instead, I put Claude in danger. I've lost the only man who truly cared about me. The man I thought I could truly love.

The man who betrayed me like Judas for a sack of silver.

I stare blankly at the flickering lights outside the window as we make our way across the city. Hope fades with every passing block. My fate is sealed and stamped.

Legally, I am bound to Nick, but my heart will forever belong to the one-armed bartender from the Black Penny.

CHAPTER SEVENTEEN
CLAUDE

She's gone. Fuck.

I stare at my reflection in the mirror behind the register. An open bottle of whiskey sits on the bar beside an empty glass. I haven't had a drink in years, but I'm close to drowning myself in whatever remains in the bottle, praying I never come up for air.

When they took her, I closed the bar, pushed everyone out. In all the years I've owned this place, I've never closed early. Not even for personal reasons.

There was always someone here. Someone to lend a listening ear, a comforting shoulder, a glass of their poison of choice. But tonight, I can't do it. I can't bear the crushing weight of my guilt. Or my pain.

A torrent of emotions swirls in my chest. I thought I had more time. When he came into the bar, my heart stopped. There was no way for me to get to her, to put myself between them before he spotted her. Once he did, it was too late.

For a weeknight, the bar was packed. If I had stepped in, someone would have been hurt. An innocent bystander caught in the crossfire. The DeLuca brothers have a reputation for being ruthless and single-minded. If they're involved, there are always casualties. I couldn't put anyone in danger.

And I sacrificed Gwen with my inaction.

My unfocused gaze blurs. I curse and swipe the tears away. Anger replaces the sadness, and I let the fire inside me rage out of control.

Someone called in her location. I knew better than to let her work at the bar. Putting her in full view of everyone left her vulnerable. I should have kept her hidden. Safe and sound. But I let her into my life, into my heart.

I rake my fingers through my hair and pull. My attention

shifts to the bottle on the bar again. The writhing agony inside leaves me longing for the numbing embrace of liquor. It'll soothe the pain, even if only temporarily.

I pour a double and cradle the glass in my hand. Who did it? Who told DeLuca where to find her? It's possible he retraced his steps from the night she first came in, but I doubt he's smart enough to realize she'd stuck around.

No, with the promise of a reward, someone called in the tip

"You gonna drink that or just let it gather dust?"

"Go away." I ignore my brother's presence, keep my attention fixed on the glass.

Grant sighs, crossing the room and sitting on the stool beside me. He takes the glass and downs the contents.

I clench my fingers into a fist.

"You've been sober for years, Claude." He pours another. "Don't fall off the wagon now."

He's right. I haven't been tempted by a drink in a long time, but tonight pushed me to the edge of the abyss. I would have gladly tumbled into it if it would have granted me relief from the torment.

The soft hum of the cooler behind the bar and the occasional click of the jukebox in the far corner are the only noises filling the void. We embrace the silence. It's familiar, comforting. We've been here before.

The night of Pap's funeral.

The morning his ex filed for divorce.

The day I was turned away from the police academy.

But none of those nights held the same weight as this…except the night I gave up drinking. The night Grant found me with a gun in my mouth and an empty bottle of whiskey at my feet. Silence filled the space between us all of that night as he sat beside me until dawn. We never spoke about it, but Grant knows the darkness inside me. The darkness I've kept at bay for years.

"When I woke up in the hospital with my hand and nearly half my arm missing, the bloody stump wrapped in bandages, I panicked." My voice carries through the empty room. "I threw off three nurses and punched a doctor. They sedated me, strapped me to the bed. It wasn't until my commanding officer came in, shouting orders, that they eased the restrictions."

Grant sips the whiskey and turns to study my profile.

I keep my gaze fixed on the register, unable to face him. "I couldn't remember anything, but my body held onto every violent memory. My commander told me what happened. How I was injured. I'm glad that part is still a blank, but it left me in pieces, mentally, emotionally…physically.

"When I came home, no one cared. Ridiculed. Cursed. Ostracized for my service to my country. Literally spit on!" I grind my teeth. "For the first two weeks, I wanted to die. I crawled into a bottle and climbed to the roof with every intent to end it."

"I remember," Grant whispers, his voice cracking.

"You saved me." I face him. "I wouldn't be here if you hadn't sat with me that night until I sobered up. You reminded me I had a place here. With you. With Pap. You promised to help."

"I did."

"You believed in me."

"I still do."

"Why?"

His jaw clenches, and he pushes aside the empty glass. "Because you're the only family I have left. The only person I can trust. You have my back, and I have yours. That's what family does. We look out for each other, believe in each other."

I nod, swallowing the lump in my throat.

"I'm sorry about Gwen." He claps his hand on my shoulder. "Quinn told me what happened. You handled it well."

"I told her to speak to her family. Make a clean break. It was her choice to make. No one else's." My fist pounds the bar. "Whoever told them where to find her stole her choice."

"Did she really have a choice, Claude?"

Grant's question is soft, but it makes me flinch, coming at me like a knife from the darkness.

"Maybe." I shake my head. "Hell, I don't know anymore."

"What *do* you know?"

Visions of Gwen fill my mind. Her smiling at me when I showed her how to make a martini. Her laughter when I taught her how to flip pancakes. Her moaning when I drove deep inside her. Her snuggling against me after we both collapsed in orgasmic bliss. There's only her consuming me, stealing my heart and filling it with joy. With love.

Without her, I'm empty, a husk of the man I was when she came into my life.

"I love her."

Grant smiles. "That's obvious."

"I can't force her to stay. She chose to go back." My heart shatters at the thought of living without her.

"What if she doesn't have a choice?"

"Everyone has a choice." I look at Grant.

"Whatever you say." He stands and tucks the bottle under his arm. "Get some sleep. I'll talk to you tomorrow."

Staring after him, I turn his question over in my mind. She doesn't have a choice…does she? After what she told me about her family and their deal with the DeLucas, there may not be anything she can do to break free.

Defeated, I retreat to my apartment and collapse on the bed. The sheets smell like sex. Her floral scent clings to the pillow, and I bury my face in it. I inhale deeply, praying I have the strength to make it through the night.

Gwen has taken possession of me, and there's not a damn thing I can do about it. She's wedged herself under my skin, imprinted her glittering presence on every part of my existence. I can't go back to the man I was before her.

She has altered the structure of my world.

And I wouldn't have it any other way.

But how can I possibly go on, now that I've tasted such happiness, only to lose it without warning?

I wrestle with my demons until exhaustion pulls me into the darkness.

CHAPTER EIGHTEEN
GWEN

The prize bird has returned to her gilded cage.

A shiver that has nothing to do with the cold ripples through me when I step into the vaulted entryway of my parent's townhome. My shoes squeak on the marble floors, damp with slush dragged in from outside.

Nick follows close behind me. His presence is suffocating. The brief moments of freedom at the Black Penny with Claude allowed me to breathe. It was like I finally broke the surface of the water, only to welcome the warm sunshine on my face and take a few gasping breaths before being dragged into the cold, dark depths once more. My situation is almost more painful after that brief taste of what could have been.

Nick takes the lead, and I don't need a guide to know where we're headed. The staircase goes to the second floor, where my parents wait in the antiquated parlor they converted to a lounge. They receive guests and conduct business there.

That's all I am. A commodity to be traded. A business deal.

Squaring my shoulders, I open the mahogany door. My mother spins away from the window at the intrusion. Her silver-threaded dark hair catches the light, and the wrinkles near her eyes and mouth seem more prominent. She looks older, more tired than I remember.

"Gwendolyn." Her smile doesn't reach her eyes.

I bristle at the use of my given name. "Mother."

"We've been so worried." She crosses the room, and for a moment, I think she's going to embrace me, but she stops short, her eyes narrowing as she takes in my appearance. "What are you wearing?" Her distaste is clear in the simple question.

I tug at the secondhand shirt Quinn and I found at the thrift shop.

"Gwendolyn Monroe." My father's voice booms through the room.

My spine stiffens. I turn to see him enter from an adjoining door. He wears every year of his age. At fifty, my father was handsome with an air of sophistication; at sixty-two, he bears a strong resemblance to an overweight, nearsighted aristocrat with a penchant for port and tobacco. He exhales a plume of smoke, still clutching the cigar between his teeth.

"Father." I hold his gaze, willing myself to stand my ground. Neither of my parents seem pleased to see me, but there's an air of relief siphoning tension from the room, as though my presence has prevented a catastrophic implosion.

"Where in the devil have you been?" my father snaps.

"I needed some time for myself." My tone is borderline antagonistic, but I stand firm. He doesn't deserve an explanation. I'm under no compulsion to give one.

His gaze shifts to Nick behind me, blocking the door. "Where did you find her?"

"At a dive bar in Hell's Kitchen." Nick's mouth curves into a sadistic grin. "She was waiting tables and making eyes at the bartender."

A scandalized gasp escapes my mother's perfect mauve lips.

I don't turn my head in her direction. My focus remains solely on my father. His brow furrows, and he pulls the cigar from between his clenched teeth.

"Did you forget your responsibility to this family?" He raises his voice just enough to emphasize his disappointment.

Years ago, I would have cowered and groveled, begged for forgiveness. But I'm not the girl I once was. I'm stronger now. Wiser.

More determined than ever to break free of my parents' hold on my life.

When I don't respond, he blusters and pushes forward. "You have a duty, and I will be damned if you ruin the reputation of this family with your selfishness."

"You don't need my help there." The response leaves my lips before I think better of it. I'm prodding the monster beneath the bed, and it's only a matter of time before it devours me whole. Desperation has made me careless.

"What did you say?" My father stands toe to toe with me, his figure looming and imposing.

I choke on the stench of his cologne and the lingering cigar smoke. He glares down his bulbous nose, taking measure of the disappointment before him.

"I'm not the one who brought this family to ruin," I say, the words breaking free. I know I'm tempting fate by putting them out into the universe. "You did that all on your own."

Pain blooms across my cheek when the back of his hand connects with my face. I stumble sideways, clutching my jaw, staring at him in horror. My father has never struck me before. I take a few steps back to put some distance between us.

"You will not speak to me like that again. Do you understand?" He growls with barely contained rage. "You are my daughter. You will do as you are told. I have arranged for you to marry Nick. You will satisfy that agreement without argument."

"And if I don't?" Defiance pushes into recklessness.

My father's eyes narrow as he puffs his cigar. The tip glows red, and the color flickers in his dark pupils. He studies me for a long moment, assessing for weaknesses, securing the best, most injurious course of action. I keep my expression blank. His satisfied grin causes gooseflesh to prickle along my arms and neck.

"I will burn down the bar where they found you, with all of your new friends inside." He sneers. "Including the bastard who kept you hidden."

A lump forms in my throat. I should have known my father would punish the innocent for my presumed crimes. The pain in my jaw radiates across my face, and my watering eyes threaten to spill over. But I refuse to give him the satisfaction of bringing me to tears, of rendering me to the penitent child he thinks I should be.

When I don't respond, he nods. "You will marry Nick in one week, and I will wash my hands of you once and for all. Am I clear?"

I bite my tongue. A sarcastic retort would only burn bridges that are barely hanging on by rotting timber and decaying rope. I can't risk angering him further, having him follow through on his threat. He would order Nick to do it without a second thought, and Nick would laugh while striking the match.

I nod. Better to placate him now than give him ammunition to hurt me later.

Silence fills the room, and I take it as my dismissal. Spinning around, I sidestep Nick and exit. My heart pounds as I race up two flights of steps to my bedroom. I ignore the servants exiting the service elevator at the back of the hallway and duck through the door, slamming it behind me.

I curse my family and Nick.

Then I curse myself for being weak. For giving in to their demands. I should have fought harder. Pushed back. But unlike my family, I have morals. There are certain lines I refuse to cross.

That's not the case for my parents. They will do whatever it takes to ensure their survival and continued success. Even if it means selling their own blood to the devil in exchange for the financial stability to maintain the illusion of their status.

A scream lodges in my throat. There's no one to help me. Nothing I can do.

I'm their prized bird in a gilded cage. My fate has already been sealed, and nothing short of an act of God will free me from this prison.

What will I do? What *can* I do?

My father will hurt those who help me, those who show me kindness and compassion. If he discovers the truth of my relationship with Claude, he'll kill him…if only to solidify my commitment to his union with the DeLuca crime family.

I need to warn Claude. But how? If I call the bar, they'll know. And I can't go to the police.

He turned me in. I should be pissed at him. But I still care. Curse my heart. I don't want him to get hurt.

I flop down onto the overstuffed bed and stare at the ceiling. I could tear my hair out. Is there anyone who can help me? Anyone who can act as a messenger?

Chewing my fingernail, I ponder the possibilities. None of the servants will help me. I wouldn't put them at risk of my father's wrath anyway. No, it has to be someone outside of the staff. Someone who isn't connected to my family. Someone who can't be bought. Someone with connections and clout.

Do I even know anyone who would put themselves at risk in such a way?

I pull myself from the bed and pace the room. My mind dismisses possibilities as quickly as it provides them. Damn it.

My gaze lands on the open door to my closet. Inside, I see gowns glittering in the dim light. I smooth my hand over the secondhand top.

Then it hits me.

Of course.

Marcy Maxwell. Stylist to the stars.

She recognized me at the bar. If anyone can help me, it's her. No one knows of her connection to the Black Penny or Claude. She's got the perfect cover. While she and my parents run in very different circles, her status as a celebrity stylist gives her clout. And they would never question my desire to hire someone to overhaul my wardrobe.

Or better yet, design my wedding gown.

A light takes shape, bright at the end of a dark tunnel. My mind forms a plan, and all I need to do is convince my mother of the immediate need for Marcy to design my gown for the upcoming wedding. This shouldn't be difficult. My mother's penchant for perfection—or at least the illusion of it—leaves her desperate. She will hire anyone I request as long as they're the best.

And Marcy Maxwell is the best in the business.

Good thing she's on my side.

Chapter Nineteen
Claude

I'm still in bed when Quinn shows up.

"What the hell is this?" She rips open the curtain, letting in sunlight and a gust of cold through the drafty windows.

I roll away from her and pull the blanket over my head. After the shit show last night, I struggled to fall asleep, but exhaustion finally overcame me around dawn. Even then, misery followed me into those few hours of sleep. I'm used to restless, sleepless nights, but this one was all in.

"Claude, get up. It's nearly noon." Quinn pokes my shoulder through the blankets.

"Go away."

"I'm not going anywhere until you get your ass out of bed and talk to me." The mattress gives under her weight as she sits beside me.

"I don't want to talk," I mumble beneath the layers of fabric.

My head hurts but less than my fucking heart. I don't want to think about Gwen or the asshole who took her away from me.

She sighs. "Are you hungry?"

"No."

"Come on." She tugs the blanket, pulling it away from my face. "You can't lay in bed all day, being a miserable wreck."

"I can and I will."

With a determined grunt, she rips the blanket off the bed. I'm fully clothed, but I shiver at the assault and her audacity. Glowering through my messy hair, I pin her with my most intimidating stare.

"Get up." She jabs my rib with her finger. "Your brother will be here any minute, and he won't be nearly as nice as me."

"Fine."

Quinn stands and smiles. "I'll go make some eggs."

I wave my hand in dismissal, anything to get her to leave me alone with my misery. When she retreats to the kitchen, I roll onto my back and stare at the ceiling.

What the hell am I doing? Moping and mooning over a woman I knew all of…what? A week? Two? I scoff. What did I think would happen? If her engagement hadn't been enough of a warning, the moment I realized who she was, I should have put a fucking electrical fence around her with a sign: *Danger. Don't sleep with her. Don't fall in love with her.*

But I didn't listen to any of the warning bells clanging in my brain. I followed my dick as it towed my heart headfirst into a fucking hurricane of heartache.

The sounds of pots clanging and running water remind me to get out of bed. Quinn won't resort to violence to get me moving, but Grant certainly will. He has before. He's worse than the boot camp sergeant who played reveille at four a.m. after we'd been running on only two hours of sleep for a week straight.

My head aches when I sit up. Part of me wishes it were a hangover, but I'm glad Grant stopped me from drowning my sorrows in that bottle of whiskey. This morning would have been worse otherwise.

I cringe at the mess I left when I crawled into bed. Clothes lay scattered around the room. For years, I kept my place neat, tidy, organized. Even when Gwen was here, I maintained order in my environment.

But now…I couldn't care less. None of it matters.

I stumble into the bathroom, turning away from the mirror. After I relieve myself and splash water on my face, I run my fingers through my hair. It sticks out, wild and relentless. There's no taming it. I give up and head to the living room.

Grant is leaning against the counter in the kitchen, speaking with Quinn. He pivots to face me when she looks up and smiles.

"Eggs are done." She scoops them from the skillet onto a plate. "Want some coffee?"

"Yeah."

Now that I'm moving, blood is flowing to my brain and my

malfunctioning heart. It hurts, not having her here. How did I become so dependent on her presence in such a short period of time? I curse myself for allowing her to burrow into my life with so little effort.

Quinn hands me a cup of coffee. "No cream, two sugars."

"Thanks." I carry it to the table.

She follows, placing the plate on the mat before me and retrieving a fork. "Need anything else?"

I shake my head and sip the coffee. It warms me, but nothing can touch the regret constricting my soul. Damn it. Is this how life is going to be from now on? Memories and regrets haunting me?

"Did you get any sleep?" Grant sits across from me.

Quinn hands him a mug of coffee as she joins us, sipping her own. Her curious attention flickers from him to me, but she remains quiet.

"Not really."

I eat the eggs even though I'm not hungry. Quinn beams with pride when I shove a forkful in my mouth.

Grant taps his fingers on the worn mug advertising a popular restaurant chain. A holdover from Pap. My brother's expression shifts, but he doesn't say anything.

"Something wrong?" I ask between bites of egg.

"Got a call from Mickey this morning. He's been doing some digging for me."

"Digging?" I shove the empty plate away and wash everything down with bittersweet coffee.

"Yeah, into Gwen's family and their ties to the DeLucas." A shadow passes in his eyes when he meets my gaze. "It's not good."

My stomach twists. "What do you mean by 'not good'?"

"He confirmed the rumors I heard yesterday. Monroe's estate is in trouble. He's made some really bad investments over the last ten years, and they're coming back to bite him in the ass." Grant shifts uncomfortably. "He's deep in bed with the DeLucas, and they're calling in favors Monroe can't guarantee. It's a dicey game. And it looks like it's been going on for a while."

"Months?"

"Try years."

"Fuck." If her family is in this much trouble, Gwen is caught smack-dab in the middle of all of it. Especially if her father sold her off to Nick DeLuca.

"That's not the worst of it." Grant clears his throat and tugs at his collar. "Oliver Monroe is under investigation for embezzlement, tax evasion, blackmail, and fraud. If he goes down, the whole family will go with him."

I shoot to my feet. "What? But Gwen doesn't know about any of this. She's innocent."

Grant stands, holding his hands out like he's trying to calm a rabid dog.

I push away from the table to pace the length of the room. "She's caught in the middle of this. If the whole thing blows up, she'll end up on trial with the rest of them." Panic rips through my chest. I should have stopped Nick. I should have kept her safe. Resting my hand on the wall, I take a breath and close my eyes. "She's innocent, Grant. She doesn't deserve this."

"Did she say anything about any of it?" he calmly asks behind me.

"No. She just wanted to get away from them…from Nick and her family." I spin to face my brother, willing him to understand. "Gwen isn't like them. She could have gone back to them, but she didn't. Not until Nick came last night."

"You don't think she wanted to go back?"

"No."

"Neither do I."

"Then how the hell did they find her?"

Grant turns. A flush of red creeps up his throat. "I called in the tip."

I stare at the man I thought I knew. "You what?" Disbelief gives way to anger. "How the fuck could you do that?"

When I rush forward and grab his shirt, he doesn't react.

Quinn races across the room and rests her hand on my arm.

"Calm down, Claude." She grips my sleeve. "Let him explain."

"You ratted her out." I stumble back, feeling like the breath has been ripped from my chest. Dueling emotions rage within me. Fury easily overcomes fear. "Why? For the reward?"

"You know me better than that." Grant rounds on me, pain etched on his face.

"Then why did you do it?" My hand pulses in a steady rhythm—fist, relax, fist, relax.

"Mickey called me yesterday morning. Monroe is making a big move, and Vice wants to nab him before he can find a way to weasel out of the charges. They have enough on him to go to trial. All they needed was a witness willing to testify."

"They found a witness." The realization leaves me reeling. "When's the arrest?"

"Tonight during a fancy dinner party Monroe is having with the DeLucas. They plan on arresting both families at once."

"Fuck." I pinch my eyes closed and try to breathe. All I can see is Gwen caught in the chaos. It's going to be a clusterfuck, and shit can go sideways fast. "Why put her in the middle of it?"

"The whole family is under investigation, Claude. If she were absent, it would look suspicious." He rubs his hand across his jaw. "All the pieces need to be in position."

"But she could get hurt. Or die." I step closer and jab my finger in my brother's chest. "I swear, if anything happens to her, I will never fucking forgive you for putting her in that position."

"That's why I didn't tell you last night." Grant holds my gaze, his familiar face a comfort and a curse in the midst of the turmoil raging inside me. "I have a plan, but you're going to have to trust me."

"How can I trust you after what you did to her?"

Grant sighs. "I know you love her, Claude. But if you want a future with this woman, you're going to have to take this risk. Please, trust me."

"How can you possibly protect her when you're on a leave of absence, recovering from an injury you sustained during a shootout in *my* bar?" I jump when Quinn takes my hand.

"It'll work out." Her smile does nothing to ease the tension inside me.

"No." I shake my head and pull away from both of them. "I'm going after her. If anyone is going to protect Gwen, it'll be me."

I rip my coat off the rack behind me and put it on. Quinn takes Grant's hand and they watch me with concern.

"Where are you going?" Grant asks, his voice stern, like when he would boss me around as a kid.

"Down to the station." I button the coat, my fingers fumbling with the narrow loops. "Who's on the case?"

"McMasters."

My head snaps up at the name. This changes everything. "Good. I'll talk to him."

"What are you going to do?" Grant looks ready to stop me, but he refrains and clutches Quinn to his side instead.

"I'm going to do what I should have done last night." I pull on my cap and head out the door.

If anything happens to Gwen, I'll never forgive myself. I will put this right.

No one touches what belongs to me. No one.

Nick DeLuca might be a feared member of a mafia family, but if my experience has taught me anything, it's to never underestimate a veteran on the warpath.

Chapter Twenty
Gwen

Convincing my mother to hire Marcy proved easier than I had anticipated. Even with the current scandal surrounding the stylist, Mother recognized Marcy's work from an event five years ago. With one well-worded request, I had her blessing.

Thankfully, the napkin Marcy gave me was still in my pocket when Nick dragged me from the bar last night. It had been washed, but I could still read the faintf numbers. After a quick, impassioned phone call, Marcy agreed to come immediately.

I fidget with the hem of my shirt. It's softer than the ones I found at the thrift store. Cashmere, of course. My mother disliked the thought of me wearing hand-me-down rags for a moment longer than necessary. With a sour look at my open closet, I take a deep breath.

Marcy will arrive any minute, but I doubt we'll be left alone together. After I ran away from Nick, my father won't take any chances of me escaping again.

I spent all night staring at the ceiling, trying to come up with a plan. A way to get a message to Claude, to warn him. Somewhere between one and three, the planning became a desperate attempt to plot my escape. Even this morning, I am no closer to devising a realistic plan to evade my father's hired thugs and Nick's henchmen. Whatever freedom I had slipped through my fingers the moment Nick caught me at the Black Penny. The window of opportunity slammed closed in my face.

A knock at the door pulls me from my dark thoughts.

"Come in." I stand, clasping my hands together to keep them from shaking.

The door opens, and I frown at the man standing there. My mood sours further when Nick steps into my room.

"What do you want?" I brace myself, anticipating an

antagonistic remark.

"Is that any way to address your future husband?" He clicks his tongue in disapproval. "Someone's here to see you." Nick steps aside to reveal another person.

"Marcy Maxwell. It's an honor." I rush forward and take her hands in mine.

She squeezes my hands, casting a glance in Nick's direction before fixing her smile on me. "It's so nice to finally meet you," Marcy gushes. "I'll admit, I was surprised when you called to ask me to design and style your wedding ensemble."

Picking up the subtle shift in her demeanor, I play along. "Well, if I'm going to get married, I should have the best stylist in the business."

She bats her lashes. "You flatter me."

I turn to Nick. "You can go."

His jaw twitches at my cool dismissal. "I'll be right outside the door." He lowers his voice and leans in close. It takes all my effort not to cringe. "In case you get any funny ideas."

Once he closes the door, I take Marcy by the hand and pull her to my closet. "Let me show you some of my ideas," I say loud enough for Nick to hear through the wall.

As soon as we reach the oversized closet, I cast one last look over her shoulder before playing my hand. "Thank you for coming."

"Of course." Her lowered tone matches mine.

"I need you to deliver a message."

Marcy snaps her gum and grins. "Good, 'cause I have one for you too."

"Wait, what?" I clap my hand over my mouth when it echoes through my room.

Marcy pulls me deeper into the closet, chattering about fabrics and popular styles to choose from. When she's sure there won't be an interruption from Nick, or anyone else, she drops her voice again.

"After we spoke this morning, I called Claude at the Black Penny. Grant answered." She thins her lips. "He told me what happened."

"Oh." The word sounds more like a squeak.

"I don't have time to explain everything, but when I told him I was coming here, he asked me to bring a message from Claude."

"Claude's the one who called in the tip." I shake my head, willing myself to remember he betrayed me. Even though I'm angry with him, I can't let my father or Nick hurt him.

Which is the whole purpose of this meeting, to send him a message. Looks like he beat me to it.

Marcy scoffs. "Not a chance, honey. Claude's more loyal than a hound dog."

"Then who?" Confusion swirls within me.

"Does it matter?" She takes me by the shoulders, and our gazes lock. "Listen, he wanted me to warn you. There's a warrant out for your parents' arrests."

I stumble back, my head drifting from side to side in slow motion. "No."

"They're coming, honey. Tonight. It'll be all over the news by morning."

Panic silences everything inside me. "What do I do?"

"Stay in your room. Keep your head down." Marcy hugs me. "They're working on a plan to get you out, but you have to stay here, in your room, for it to work."

Her whispered words do nothing to ease the fear churning in the pit of my gut.

"If they come, it'll get ugly." I stare at her in horror, knowing exactly how Nick will respond to a police raid. "People will die."

"I know, honey." She squeezes my hand. "That's why you need to lock your door and hide if you hear *anything*."

"We're having a huge dinner tonight," I stammer. "It was supposed to be a business thing, but now they want to celebrate the upcoming wedding."

"I suggest you find a way to miss it."

A million thoughts bombard me at once. I don't know how I'm going to get out of this, especially since I'm one of the guests of honor.

Shit. My parents are going to lose it if I bail.

A light forms at the end of the tunnel. This is my out. My opportunity to escape for good. With my parents arrested, I'll be free. A breath of pure relief escapes me before reality crashes down again. What if they arrest *me*? Just like that, the panic returns.

"This gown is lovely. A Versace? I'm totally jealous." Marcy laughs, and I mimic her. "I love your suggestions. Shall we take your measurements then? I can start the hunt for the perfect dress today."

My mind spins with information while Marcy pulls a measuring tape from a bag on her hip. She leads me back to the bedroom and takes my measurements, jotting them down on a small notepad. I follow her lead, all the while thinking about the implications of her message.

Claude didn't sell me out.

He's worried about me.

He wants me.

Does this mean he loves me?

I bite my lip as worry consumes me once more. How the hell am I going to avoid this dinner? I can't get caught in the middle of this disaster. I can't imagine how bad it would have been if she hadn't warned me.

"I've got everything I need to get started." She puts the notes and the tape back in her bag. Her voice lowers, carrying only between the two of us. "What's the message?"

"Huh?" I blink at her before I remember the whole purpose of having her come today. "Oh yeah. Tell Claude..." The original message I'd planned to send dies on my lips, replaced by a simpler one. "Tell him to be careful."

A grin splits Marcy's mauve lips. "Sugar, you don't have to worry about him. He can take care of himself just fine."

"Thanks, Marcy. I owe you one."

She laughs and crosses the room. Opening the door, she turns to face me, ignoring the imposing presence of Nick and his thugs behind her. She winks at me. "You be sure to tell everyone you were styled by Marcy Maxwell, and we'll call it even."

"Are you done?" Nick snaps.

"I've got everything I need to find the perfect wedding gown," she purrs. "You're a lucky man. Ciao!" With a wave, she walks down the hall.

"Escort her out," Nick growls to his goons. They rush forward and disappear down the hall, leaving us alone.

I fold my arms across my chest and hold his stare when he refuses to leave. "What?"

"Enjoy your freedom while it lasts." His grin borders on sadistic as he pulls the door closed.

What does he mean by that? *Freedom?* What freedom?

Then it hits me. The tiny strands of glittering freedom I have under my parents' roof will disappear completely when I'm his wife.

I stumble back and collapse on the bed. Grabbing the fluffy pillow in the center, I hug it to my chest like a shield.

There's nothing in this world that can protect me from my fate.

In the back of my mind, Marcy's message rings clear like a church bell on Christmas morning. *They're coming. Tonight. Keep your head down.*

Hope shines like a beacon in darkness. A flickering candle in a storm. If there's any possibility of escape, it will come in the midst of the chaos. I only hope I don't find myself trapped in an even worse position.

Married to Nick.

Arrested.

Dead.

CHAPTER TWENTY-ONE
CLAUDE

What the hell am I doing? It doesn't matter. I need to protect Gwen.

When I'm halfway out the door, Grant stops me. "Wait."

"What?" I turn, glaring at him. After what he did, I'm not sure I can trust his judgment. He wasn't wrong…but at the same time, I can't believe he let Gwen go back to that house knowing what awaited her.

"I'll come with you." He grabs the extra coat beside the door. "Maybe I can grease the wheels with McMasters."

Begrudgingly, I concede. If anyone can convince McMasters to let me tag along, it's my brother. They went to the academy together and have known each other for years. When I tried to join the force, McMasters tried to talk me out of it. After they denied my entrance to the academy, he never said, "I told you so." I haven't seen him in years.

Grant kisses Quinn, and I turn away, unable to bear a press of pain at the simple, loving gesture.

When I step into the hallway, my brother trails behind. Silence stretches between us like an old, weathered rubber band. Cold December air bites my skin, making me bundle deeper into the flannel-lined jacket.

The moment we fall into step outside, the tension snaps with a soft muttered curse from Grant.

"Why are you really coming?" I glance at him out of the corner of my eye. Grant has always been an overprotective older brother, but lately, he's been even more paternal than usual.

"Because you need someone in your corner."

I snort and turn my attention to the clustered groups of pedestrians in our path. "If you were really in my corner, you wouldn't have turned her in."

"You're right." He sighs and shoves his hands into his pockets. "I shouldn't have sent in the tip without telling you."

"Doesn't matter now." I focus on what's in front of me instead of dwelling on the past.

"It *does* matter."

We cross the street, and I'm too wrapped up in my own thoughts to respond.

"Claude." He reaches out and grabs the sleeve of my jacket.

I pull up short, stopping just before I collide with a tall man in a navy peacoat. "What?"

"It matters." He steps closer, and the foot traffic moves around us as we stand still at the corner. "You're the only family I have left. I can't…" His voice cracks.

I rest my hand on his shoulder. "I'm not going anywhere, Grant."

"I know but…" He takes a deep breath. "You love her, and if this shit goes sideways, I…"

The unspoken implication hangs in the air between us.

"I'm stronger now," I say. "I'm not the man I was then."

He nods, and the helpless fear in his eyes kicks me in the gut.

"I love her, and I'm going to do whatever I need to do to make sure she's safe." Quinn's face appears in my mind, and a flash of gunfire in my memory takes me back to August when I thought I lost my brother. He nearly sacrificed himself for the woman he loves. "You understand."

"I do." He releases me and sighs. "Let's go talk to McMasters."

Tension builds with every step.

When we reach the station, my brother turns to me. "Let me do the talking, okay?"

I shrug. There's no way I can make that promise.

With a shake of his head, Grant leads the way into the building, greeting everyone as he passes. By the time we step onto the fourth floor, he's spoken to half the building. I didn't realize how loved my brother was in the department, but I'm not surprised.

McMasters stands when we walk into the office, and he shakes Grant's hand. "Richards, what the hell are you doing here? I thought you were recovering."

"I am." Grant steps aside. "We needed to talk to you."

"McMasters." I offer my hand, which he takes without hesitation.

"Claude." He rests, half-seated on the edge of his desk. "What can I do for you?"

"You're working the Monroe case, right?" Grant lowers his voice, keeping the conversation between us.

"Yeah." His gaze shifts from me to Grant. "What about it?"

"You're planning to take him down tonight?"

McMasters narrows his eyes. "Yeah. Why?"

"I want in." I speak before I can second-guess myself.

He scoffs. "You're not a cop, Claude. You know I can't let you do that."

"I need to be there." I hold my ground. I don't waver. My hand clenches into a fist.

"Why?" McMasters crosses his arms.

"The daughter. She's innocent."

"She's not the target."

"Yes, but she's in the home. If shit goes sideways, she'll be caught in the crossfire."

McMasters scowls. "What makes you think this won't be a clean arrest?"

"Because Nick DeLuca is her fiancé. If there's a raid, he won't go down without a fight," I say.

If McMasters has done his research, he already knows this. But I can't take the chance he doesn't.

"And he'll take her down with him."

"Why would he do that?"

"Because he's a sadistic bastard who doesn't care who he hurts as long as he gets what he wants." I straighten, flexing my fingers, imagining them wrapped around DeLuca's throat.

"Why do you want to get involved?" McMasters's stare burns a hole straight through to my soul.

"She's mine."

McMasters's brows shoot into his hairline. "She's engaged to DeLuca."

"Not anymore." My voice rings with certainty and purpose. "Gwen is being held against her will."

"Do you have proof of that?" He rolls his shoulders and stands.

I quickly relay the events of that snowy night and the subsequent information she told me concerning her parents and Nick DeLuca. Most of it doesn't seem to surprise McMasters, but he's stunned to see me so impassioned.

"I love her, and if you don't let me protect her, you'd better not get in my way."

He chokes on his coffee. "I can't give you a badge and a gun for a day, Claude. That's not how this works."

"Then don't. But I'm going tonight, with or without your blessing."

"I don't want to arrest you for obstruction."

"I won't obstruct. I'll be in and out, five minutes." Purpose fills me. "Gwen needs me."

"I can send in a team to make sure the girl is safe." McMasters strokes his jaw. "Make sure no harm comes to her."

"Put me on it."

"I *can't* do that, Claude."

"Then let me do it." Grant speaks up, and I turn, stunned. "I'll go with a small team. In and out. Ten minutes, tops. Let you focus on Monroe and DeLuca."

"I don't know, Richards." He shakes his head. "You're still recovering from a gunshot wound. You haven't been cleared for duty."

"I can handle it." Grant nods, pressing his lips together in a thin line.

McMasters's gaze passes from Grant to me and back again before he exhales sharply. "Fine. Come into the briefing room. I'll get you up to speed."

I move to follow them, but McMasters holds up his hand. "Not you, Claude. We can handle this."

I grit my teeth, let the irritation simmer into oblivion.

"Fine."

A plan forms in my mind, but I keep it close, not willing to dwell on it yet.

Instead, I leave the station to head back home. The brisk chill steals some of my irritation, but I'm still smoldering when I reach the bar. Inside, I slam the door and head for the office. My head hurts. I rest it on the desk.

A volatile combination of emotions rages through me, each one warring for control. I'm two seconds from breaking every rule I've ever made for myself and storming across town to single-handedly bust down Monroe's door.

The phone rings.

"Hello?"

"Claude, thank God. It's Marcy."

"Marcy?" Confusion fills me. Why would she call me? "What's wrong?"

"Gwen called me. She hired me as her stylist. I just got back from seeing her."

"Is she okay?" Hope unfurls in my chest.

"She's fine." She sighs. "I gave her the message your brother asked me to deliver."

Grant spoke to Marcy? I close my eyes and shake my head.

"I called to talk to you, but he answered. Told me to warn her."

A slim thread of relief eases into my mind. "Good."

"She asked me to deliver a message to you."

My heart pounds. "What's the message?"

"Be careful and don't do anything stupid."

"Those are her exact words?"

"I added the last part." Marcy's tone softens. "You love her, Claude. Don't fuck this up."

"I won't. Thanks, Marcy."

A ragged sense of purpose fills me as I hang up the phone.

I have one shot at saving her, and it needs to count.

Carefully, I pull out the pistol I keep in the bottom drawer of my desk. The one Pap gave me when I came home from Vietnam.

The one I swore I would never touch again.

CHAPTER TWENTY-TWO
GWEN

I'm going to puke.

It took me an hour to convince my mother I was too sick to attend the dinner. After my visit with Marcy, I concocted a plan to ensure I would remain in my bedroom for the duration of the evening. This might be the most reckless thing I've ever done, but I can't take any chances. Not when I know what my family, what Nick, is capable of. When the police arrive, all hell will break loose.

I have no idea when the police will arrive or what exactly will happen when they do. But I played my part. Wrapping myself under the blankets, I moaned and shivered.

Mother attempted to drag me from the bed, and I collapsed, clutched my stomach, writhed on the floor. She prodded my face and threatened to call a doctor. When I refused to budge, she threw her hands in the air and retreated to the bathroom for a bottle of aspirin.

She tapped her foot while I climbed back into bed, clutching the bottle in her perfectly manicured fingers and frowning at my sorry state. With a huff of impatience, she tossed the bottle onto the blanket and told me to come down by seven-thirty.

That was an hour ago. It's now seven.

Someone should give me an Oscar for my performance, but it won't be enough. My mother doesn't care if I'm at death's door. She wants me present. If I don't show up, she'll pull me from bed and drag me down the stairs to parade me in front of her guests. I'm the guest of honor, after all. Without me, who can my parents use as a glittering distraction? My stomach churns at the thought of being put on display. I'd rather die than be subjected to that torment for another moment. I can only pray the police arrive before my clock runs out.

I chew my fingernail and watch the clock beside my bed. Five minutes after seven. Cocktails started at six-thirty. If I don't dress and join them, my father will ensure Nick punishes me for disregarding their instructions.

And I know what kind of twisted asshole Nick really is.

My cuticle bleeds when I rip the nail too short. Shit. I grab a tissue to staunch the bleeding, then rush to the bathroom and wrap my finger in a bandage.

I catch a glimpse of myself in the mirror. What the hell am I doing? This isn't going to end well. Even if Claude finds a way to save me, it'll be too late. I'll be caught up in this mess, and they'll never be able to untangle me from the hell my parents have created.

It's over. I might as well embrace the inevitable. No matter what happens tonight, I'm fucked.

My cheeks are pale, and I look sick. Which helps my case, but it's not a stomach virus that has me in its clutches. It's my inevitable fate. Too bad Marcy couldn't smuggle me out of the house in her bag.

Nick's kept a close eye on me all day. Something that wouldn't have bothered me a few years ago, but now I know better. I want nothing to do with him. I'd be better off throwing myself from the fourth-floor window than following through with this farce of a marriage. He doesn't love me. He doesn't want me. I'm a commodity. A means to an end.

He's nothing like Claude. No one is.

A tear slips free, and I wipe it away with a sniff.

"He's not coming for you." My voice echoes off the bathroom tiles, as if I'm in a stone tomb, and a piece of my soul dies. "Stop dreaming."

Somehow, I manage to scrape together what remains of my sanity and take a breath. Maybe I can find a way out of the house while everyone is at dinner. No one will be watching my door, not with such prestigious guests in the house. I stash a few items in a bag and sling it over my shoulder. The sentimental tidbits hidden in a box under my sink are now tucked into an old bag on my hip.

I hope this works. It's my last chance to escape. With a deep breath, I stiffen my resolve. I can do this. I have to do this. Or I'll die trying.

I'm halfway across the room when the door bursts open, the wood splintering where the lock broke free under the force of the impact. It knocks me back, and I nearly lose my balance.

Bracing myself against the bedpost, I search for somewhere to hide. There's nowhere. I look again, and this time my gaze stops at the doorway.

Nick, eyes wild, hair standing on end, fills the space. The gun in his hand glints in the soft light. With a growl, he grips it tighter before leveling it at me.

My knees buckle, but I grip the post tighter to remain standing. I won't surrender to this bastard. Not now. Not ever.

"What are you doing?" I hate that my voice shakes, but the barrel of the gun aimed in my direction leaves my courage in a puddle on the floor.

"Shut the fuck up." He steps into my room, his aim steady. "If I'm going down, I'm taking you with me."

"I don't understand." I scramble backward, trying to keep some distance between us. He closes the gap, and I can make out the letters on the barrel of the gun when he stops.

"Come here," he growls and grabs my arm, pulling me against him and dragging me to the door. "Let's go."

"Where are you taking me?" My hands tremble as he hauls me down the hallway toward the back staircase.

He scoffs. "Where I should've taken you the night I pulled your ass from that bar."

"I don't understand what's going on."

He shoves me down the stairs, keeping a firm hold on my arm, the gun digging into my spine. "You'll figure it out soon enough. I need to get you out of here before the cops show up."

Fear trails its fingers over my heart. "What?"

"Got an inside tip. The cops are gonna crash our party. But they won't find either of us there." He chuckles, and the sound rips hope from my soul. "We'll be long gone."

Nick motions for me to open the door. I do it slowly, trying to find a way to break free from his hold, to escape. But there's no one in the street behind the house. Empty, frosted car windows stare back at me like vacant eyes from either side of the street.

The cold air bites my bare arms, and the padded slippers on my feet do nothing to stop the damp from seeping between my toes, numbing them.

A car appears at the end of the street. Hope flares in my chest. Maybe it's the cops!

When it comes to a stop in front of us, Nick shoves me forward. "Get in."

Damn it. I cast another panicked glance down the street, praying someone is there to see us.

"I said get in the fucking car!" He pushes me, and I stumble, pitching into the backseat.

By the time I right myself, he's seated beside me and the car is in motion.

I flop down into the seat and push my hair out of my face. "Why are you doing this?"

Nick turns, once again leveling the gun in my direction. Desperation glints in his eyes as he tightens his grip on the weapon. "You sold us out, you vicious little bitch."

"I…I didn't…"

"That's why you ran." He bares his teeth like a rabid dog, cornered and scared. "You knew they were coming for us and sold us out."

"No…I…" I shrink back, wishing I had run, had left the city when I had the chance.

"You fucking ran to the cops and spilled your guts." He presses the gun to my head.

The cold barrel digs into my scalp. Tears fill my eyes. Fear steals my breath. "I didn't say anything."

"You fucking lie. Don't fucking lie to me!"

"I'm not lying!" I choke on the sobs lodged in my throat. Part of me wants him to pull the trigger, to end my suffering. But if I relent—if I give in—he wins.

He's winning regardless. I'm trapped in this car, at gunpoint, with no possible means of escape. No one knows where I am.

No one.

Nick pulls back and the pressure of the cold barrel disappears. "It doesn't matter. Not anymore."

"Why are you doing this?" A sob breaks free, cracking the remaining fragments of my sanity.

"Your father and I had an agreement," he hisses. "You are mine, and I'm taking what I'm owed."

"You'll never get away with it. They'll look for me. They'll never stop searching for me."

His laughter makes my blood run cold.

"I've already taken care of it."

"What do you mean?" My voice catches.

"The cops won't find us at the little party your parents organized." His sadistic grin flashes beneath a passing street light. "They'll find our *remains*, barely recognizable, at my apartment uptown. *A desperate pair of star-crossed lovers take their lives.*"

I cringe at the reference to Romeo and Juliet. "No one will believe it."

"They will. Because they were well compensated to believe it." He rests the gun on his thigh, his finger still on the trigger. "Our new identities will be ready by the end of the month. All we need to do is lay low."

"And then what?" I snap, ignoring the weapon. If he wanted to kill me, he would have done so already. "You're delusional if you think I'll become your docile little wife."

"I'm sure you'll come around after a while." He relaxes against the leather seat.

"I'm not a dog to be housebroken." I stiffen at his glare. "You might as well kill me now and be done with it."

"What a waste that would be." He snickers. "Now that we're both officially dead, I can take my time, make sure you're properly trained to follow my instructions."

My empty stomach lurches at the implication of his words. I turn and stare out the window at the passing city. *Claude.* His name repeats in my mind, over and over. A silent prayer. A desperate plea. Tears spill free, and I pinch my eyes closed, finally caving to the reality of my situation. It's over. Nick won. There's no one coming to save me.

Thirty minutes later, we pull up to an abandoned warehouse, near the bay. It's hard to tell exactly where we are in the darkness. I don't recognize this part of the city. A lone light flickers in an upstairs window of the two-story brick building.

"Welcome home, sweetheart." Nick grabs my arm and pulls me from the car.

I trip over my feet when I finally break free of the car. He tightens his hold on my arm, leveling the gun at my chest.

The driver takes off without a word, leaving the two of us in a dark, narrow stretch between abandoned warehouses. I jerk my arm free and straighten my back.

"Don't even think about running." He sneers.

"Where the hell would I go, moron?"

He grabs my face in his hand and squeezes. "First lesson. Don't talk back."

His hand connects with my cheek.

The sting leaves me reeling.

I step out of his reach and cradle my face in my hand.

"Let's go." He gestures to the warehouse with the barrel of the gun. "Traitors first."

Keeping distance between us, I push open the door and step into a dark, open space. An overhead lamp flicks on, flooding the room with light. There's nothing but a table and a few chairs tucked in the corner. Along the far wall, a staircase leads to the second floor, where I saw the light shining from outside.

"Upstairs. Move it." He nudges me with the pistol, and I spin, grabbing a chair and placing it between us.

"I'd rather die." Strength returns to my voice. This is my stand.

"Pity." He levels the gun at my head.

I close my eyes and take a deep breath. Peace fills me as I exhale. This is the end of the line.

"Put down the gun, DeLuca." The voice booms through the open space.

My eyes fly open, hope spears my heart. I turn toward the sound, mindful of Nick's gun still trained on me.

"Well, well." Nick licks his lips and turns, the gun still firm in his grip. He narrows his eyes at the intruder in the doorway. "What do we have here?"

"You're under arrest."

Nick's laughter echoes through the warehouse. "I don't think so."

"Let her go."

"What are you gonna do about it?"

The figure in the doorway steps into view, and I suck in a breath. Grant! The similarity in his features has me choking with emotion. For a moment, I thought it was Claude, but he's not a cop. He's not coming to save me.

Disappointment dilutes the adrenaline coursing through my body. I cling to the chair, wishing I could disappear into the darkness outside.

Grant's gaze remains solely on the man before him. "There's no way out of this, DeLuca. Put down the gun and come quietly."

"Or what? You'll shoot me?" He laughs, and I shiver at the cold, disturbing sound.

"Your only way out of here is in cuffs or a body bag." Grant's voice oozes confidence. "Pick one."

"You sure about that, pig?"

Grant's eye twitches, but he remains steadfast and only nods.

"If I'm going down, then this bitch goes first." Nick swings his arm wide, aiming the gun in my direction. He squeezes the trigger, a grin on his disgusting lips.

I hold my breath and close my eyes.

Gunfire echoes through the warehouse.

I brace for impact.

It never comes.

My eyes fly open to see Nick stumble toward me. The gun falls from his hand, clattering to the concrete. Red blooms across his chest as he staggers, blood seeping through his dark blue shirt. He lunges at me, catching me by the waist and dragging me to the floor as he collapses. His blood, warm and sticky, seeps through my cashmere shirt.

Panic seizes me, and I shove him away, scrambling backward. I'm filled with horror at the sight of Nick at my feet, his vacant eyes wide with surprise. I climb to my feet and spin around to find Grant, his gun at his side, his attention focused over his shoulder, a scowl on his face.

A second man steps into view with a pistol in his hand, smoke drifting from the barrel. The familiar curve of his profile mirrors Grant's.

"Claude?" Relief and disbelief pour through me.

He passes the gun to his brother and rushes to my side, dropping to his knees beside me. Without a word, he gathers me to his chest and holds me close.

"Are you all right?" he asks, his hand skimming over my bloodstained shirt.

I nod, unable to find my voice. Finally, I'm safe. He came for me. I close my eyes and rest in his embrace.

"Get her out of here." Grant's statement makes me look up. "I'll take care of this mess."

Claude slowly stands before offering me his hand. I take it and burrow myself into his side, wrapping my arm around his waist.

"Are you sure about this?" Claude asks, stopping beside his brother.

"Yeah." Grant sets his jaw. "Now go."

"Grant—"

His brother sighs. "Go. Now. Cyril will take you home, then come back for me."

With a nod, Claude leads me from the warehouse. Outside, I curl into his warmth. A black town car pulls up and the driver emerges.

He opens the back door. "Sir."

"Thanks, Cyril," Claude acknowledges the driver with a smile and helps me into the car. Safely inside, he closes the door, and moments later, we're speeding across town.

He pulls me into his lap and cradles me against his chest.

It's over. All of it. Nick is dead. My parents have been arrested. What the hell will happen to me now?

I sob, and Claude says nothing. He just holds me tighter.

Chapter Twenty-Three
Claude

She's safe.

Safe.

The word repeats, over and over, in my mind. Even though she's cradled against me and I can feel every breath, the adrenaline won't recede.

Seeing her with a gun pressed to her head pushed me over the edge. I promised to remain out of sight, out of the way. But then I heard that manic edge to his voice, desperation in every word.

Grant's going to be pissed. I left a mess for him to clean up. Whatever happens, I'll take the heat for it. In my mind, it's worth sacrificing my own freedom to ensure Gwen's. Even if that means we can't be together.

She shivers against me, and I shove my thoughts aside. I'll worry about consequences later. Right now, I need to take care of her.

I gently stroke her hair and press soft kisses to the top of her head. She curls deeper into me. Her soft sobs cut through the silence. I close my eyes and hold her close. It's over.

Cyril turns a sharp corner with ease, and I look at him in the rearview mirror. He's focused on the road. I don't know what I would have done without him tonight. How I would have gotten her home. I'm forever in Arthur's debt for sending his driver to our aid.

When Grant returned from the station, he found me in the office with Pap's pistol in my hand. He confronted me in that irritating, older-brother-knows-best way. But I wasn't about to leave Gwen's life to the fickle wheel of fate. I was going to save the woman I love, with or without his help.

After five minutes of swearing and dredging up our past

missteps, he conceded. While he agreed with McMasters that I shouldn't be a part of the raid, he wasn't going to say anything if I just showed up. But there was a catch.

I had to let him handle any problems.

An hour later, Rob and Arthur showed up, offering their support and whatever resources they could, including a car and driver, should we need them.

Our plan had been to get Gwen out while the rest of the party focused on the arrests. We hadn't counted on Nick DeLuca ducking out of the festivities and threatening to kill Gwen.

That isn't entirely true. I knew he would try to take her down. Possessive assholes like him love to show their cards, even while pretending they're bluffing.

Grant and I found the door ajar, but he made me stay back. Stay quiet. I could never do that while the woman I love is in danger.

Cyril passes the Black Penny and turns down a narrow street, stopping beside the side entrance. He climbs from the driver's seat and rounds the car.

"Come on, sweetheart." I nudge Gwen. "Let's go upstairs."

She pulls away and blinks up at me. Her eyes are bloodshot. Smears of blood stain her pale skin. She nods and follows when I step from the car.

I give Cyril a tight smile as I wrap my arm around Gwen. He tips his hat and closes the door before returning to the driver's seat.

Inside, the sound of music and conversation drifts from the bar. I ignore it and lead Gwen up the stairs to my apartment.

She doesn't cower or hide. She stands tall, tucked under my arm, as we climb the staircase. One hand clings to the front of my jacket while the other tightens around my waist.

I release her for a brief moment to unlock the door.

Gwen steps into my apartment and turns to face me. Questions swim in her eyes, but she doesn't voice them. She will when she's ready.

"Let's get you cleaned up." I take her hand and lead her to the bathroom.

"I can do it." She swats my hand away when I reach for the buttons of her blood-soaked sweater.

I lean against the counter and watch, my heart swelling at the sight of her, safe and whole. She's mine. I shouldn't react this way, not after what happened tonight. But I can't control how she makes me feel. How hungry I am for her. It feels like weeks since I've kissed her, since I've been inside her. When she pushes her pants down over her hips, I pivot away and turn on the shower.

Running water fills the silence. A gentle pressure surrounds me as Gwen wraps her arms around my waist and rests her face on my back. I freeze, hand braced against the wall beside the shower. She holds me, not moving for several moments.

When she shifts her weight, her hand drops to the top of my jeans. I hold my breath as she unfastens them and pushes the fabric down my hips.

"Gwen." I turn, but my brain stops functioning when I meet her luminous blue eyes.

"Join me."

She cups my balls, and all rational thought flies from my head.

I manage to push her away long enough to remove my clothes before ushering her into the shower. Under the warm spray, she embraces me, pressing her body into mine. Her hands roam over my skin.

I distract myself with the washcloth, soaping it up, washing the blood from her face and neck. She turns, letting me worship her with the suds.

The bloody memories disappear down the drain, leaving the two of us wet and clinging to each other.

"Claude," she whimpers, pressing back into me.

The cloth falls from my hand. I grip her thigh, letting my fingertips dance across her skin. When they brush the folds of her pussy, she arches into my hand.

"I want you," she gasps. "Please."

With a growl, I spin her around and hook my hand behind her knee. Pressing her against the wall, I lift her leg, and she opens for me. Her hand wraps around my cock, pushing the head to where she craves it.

I slide deep, and our mingled groans of pleasure echo off the tile.

She grips my arms, holding tight as I drive into her. Her sharp nails bite my skin. Her hips move in tandem with each thrust, meeting me with her own desperate need.

I grind against her, teasing her clit with every stroke.

She moans and throws her head back, biting her lip.

With all my effort, I pour myself into driving the demons from her mind. From her past. From my past.

Together, like this, there's nothing else. Just pure bliss. Utter abandon.

"Yes, more. More."

Her cries push me over the edge.

I wrangle myself under control long enough to feel her tighten around me. She buries her face against my chest as the orgasm ripples through her limbs. Shortly after, I come with a groan, letting our mingled mess rinse away under the shower.

It takes a minute before I can move again. She carefully disentangles herself from me and cleans us both before turning off the water.

Gwen stands on her tiptoes, kissing me softly. "Thank you."

I nod, unable to speak. My chest tightens. How can I love her so damn much it hurts?

Wrapped in a towel, she retreats to the bedroom. I follow and wrap my arm around her waist, pulling her onto the bed. I tug the blanket over us and inhale her sweet scent.

My hand rests on her heart, and slowly, the world fades into the background.

"Claude." Her voice cracks.

"Mm-hmm?" I tighten my hold on her.

"Thank you."

"For what?"

"Coming to my rescue."

"I'm sorry I didn't come sooner."

She shakes her head. "No. I'm sorry. I shouldn't have

dragged you into this mess."

"Gwen, look at me." I tip her chin until she rolls over. Our eyes lock. "I will always come for you. I love you."

Tears form in her wide sapphire eyes. "I love you too."

I brush her damp hair back and smile. My heart expands at her simple confession.

"What happens now?" She chews on her lower lip.

"That's up to you." I stroke her jaw with my thumb.

"What do you mean?" Her brow furrows.

"Well, you can go to trial, testify against your family, or…" I pause, gauging her reaction. "We'll figure it out."

Gwen cups my cheek in her hand. "What if I just want *you*?"

"You have me either way."

She wraps her legs around me, rubbing herself against my thigh. I groan.

"Then let's start over," she says.

"You're willing to leave the past behind you?"

"Yes." With a sigh, she sinks into me. Our lips meet, and I'm lost in her once more.

This time I make love to her, savoring the moment, the woman I adore.

After she drifts off to sleep, sated from another orgasm, I slip from the bed and pull on my robe. I close the bedroom door behind me and pick up the phone.

"It's me. She's safe. What's the plan?" I lean against the wall and wait for Grant to fill me in. He tells me they caught Nick's goons, who confessed to his plan—them pretending to be dead, the new identities, the works.

A plan forms in my mind even as a weight lifts from my shoulders. When I hang up the phone, there's a renewed sense of peace. Of finality.

I climb back into bed, pulling her against me, locking her into place.

Nothing will take her from me again. She's right where she's meant to be.

CHAPTER TWENTY-FOUR
GWEN

I wake in an empty but familiar bed.

Slowly, the events of the night before filter to my consciousness. I shiver at the horrifying memories of Nick holding a gun to my head. His threats echo through my mind, like the haunting strains of a horror movie soundtrack.

Pulling the blanket around my bare shoulders, I scan the dim room. Where is Claude? It's morning, barely. He should be beside me, but the bed is empty and cold.

When he came to my rescue last night, everything else fell away. He saved me. He pulled the trigger on the one man who held my life in an iron fist. I shouldn't have doubted he would find a way. Not that I need a knight in shining armor, but last night, the presence of one certainly tipped the scales in my favor.

I had always known Nick was crazy, but I never dreamed he would take it to that extreme. I *should* have known. He was a ticking timebomb. I'm glad it's over.

But is it really?

Noise drifts through the door from the living room. I wrap myself in the blanket and creep across the floor. I crack open the bedroom door before sagging with relief.

Claude sits on the couch while the television flickers against the far wall. His furrowed brow and compressed lips tell me something's wrong. Quietly, I open the door and cross the room, dragging the blanket like a cape wrapped around my shoulders.

He glances at me when I flop on the couch beside him. His countenance brightens when I lean against him.

"Did the television wake you?" he asks, taking my hand in his.

"No." I shiver dramatically. "I got cold."

"Sorry, sweetheart." He wraps his arm around me and

draws me closer. "Shall we go back to bed?"

"What are you watching?" I gesture to the television, barely registering the scrolling text at the bottom of the screen.

Claude sighs and turns up the volume.

"Veronica and Oliver Monroe were arrested in their home yesterday evening. Their ties to the DeLuca crime family have been under investigation for the last year." The blonde newswoman reads the script over images of the front steps of my family home, my parents being led away in cuffs bathed in flashing red-and-blue lights.

My stomach twists and I watch in horror as the scene unfolds on the screen. Claude holds me close, silent and supportive.

"Unfortunately, this has also been a tragic turn of events. Authorities have confirmed the daughter of Oliver Monroe, beloved socialite Gigi Monroe, has died at the age of twenty-nine. She was killed by Nick DeLuca before he took his own life."

My jaw drops open, and I turn to Claude, who seems unsurprised by the announcement. His attention shifts to me.

"Did she just say I *died?*"

"Yes."

"And that Nick killed himself after he killed me?"

"Mm-hmm." Claude nods thoughtfully.

"The bastard actually pulled it off." I study Claude's face. "You don't seem surprised."

"Grant told me last night. Nick's goons confessed his plan. Grant told the officials both you and Nick were found dead. End of story." A soft smile curves his lips. "You're a free woman."

I blink twice before it fully registers. I'm free. The pang of sadness over the loss of my past shifts into a grander spectrum, full of bright colors and unlimited possibilities. My heart soars.

"I'm free." I say the words in a reverent whisper, almost afraid to break the spell granting me the new beginning I've craved for years.

Claude kisses my temple.

"What does this mean?" I ask, looking up at him.

"It means you can do whatever you want. Be whoever you want."

Whoever I want? I shift and straddle his lap, the blanket tangling around us, pulling low to expose my shoulder. He meets me, eye to eye, his hand resting on my hip over the fabric.

I search his handsome face, admire the sharp angles and faded scars. When I walked into the bar that snowy night, I sought refuge, safety, escape. He came to my rescue when I needed him. He offered a bloody stranger a place to stay, a chance to escape. No questions asked, demanded nothing in return. Everything I gave him, I did out of gratitude…and out of love.

When I reach up to cup his cheek, the blanket slips, pooling around my waist. His jaw tightens under my touch. Warmth sinks into me, and the pieces fall into place.

I know what I want. And who.

"Claude." I lick my lips and lean into him. My breasts press against the soft fabric of his tee shirt. "Did you mean what you said last night?"

"What did I say?"

"You love me."

"Of course." He grins. "I fell in love with you the moment you walked into my bar."

Heat blooms in the pit of my stomach and radiates outward. "That fast, huh?"

"Yeah." Pink infuses his cheeks. "I guess that sounds crazy."

"Not crazy." I wrap my arms around his neck, resting my forearms on his shoulders. "I fell for you that night too."

"Did you really?" he asks, arching his brow.

"God's honest truth."

"Is that why you asked to stay with me?"

"Maybe." Heat singes my cheeks at the confession. "I thought you were handsome…and sweet."

"Sweet?" He chuckles. "Never heard that before."

"Well, you are."

Claude tosses aside the blanket, leaving me bare in his lap. I shiver at the glint of hunger in his eyes. He slides his hand over my hip, down to where my thigh meets my ass. His long fingers tease the seam of my pussy, nudging me closer.

I rock against him and moan. My fingers thread through his hair.

He slides two fingers into me, then removes them. When he brings the digits to his lips and tastes my arousal, I whimper.

"You're the sweet one." Claude grins and lays me on the couch. He drapes one of my legs over his shoulder while the other hangs off the side. I catch a flash of his teeth before he buries his face between my thighs.

The first swipe of his tongue against my clit is pure bliss. I roll my hips and bury my fingers in his hair. He fucks me with his tongue, devouring me, watching my reaction. I surrender completely and cry out when he sucks my clit, rolling it with his tongue.

"Claude, please," I beg as my body tenses.

He blows across my sensitive nub, and I buck in response. Before I can catch my breath, he thrusts two fingers deep and covers me with his mouth. The flat of his tongue puts pressure on my clit as he thrusts, over and over, with his fingers. The climax hovering just out of reach slams into me with the force of a runaway train.

I scream his name. My panting whimpers drown out the television as waves of pleasure ebb through my limbs. I sink deeper into the couch, unable to move, let alone think.

Claude's soft laughter brings me back to reality. I open my eyes to find him kneeling between my legs, grinning at me.

"That's not fair." I pout.

"What?" He settles back against the couch as I slowly climb to my feet.

My body still humming from the orgasm he gave me, I kneel and palm him through his sweatpants. His head falls back against the sofa as I tug the fabric down.

"Gwen, you don't…" His protest dies with a moan as I take him deep into my mouth.

I fist the base of his cock with my hand. When I suck the

head, I stroke. The sounds coming from deep in his throat spur me on.

I'm dripping wet, but I've never felt more powerful, more in control. So I keep going, letting him thrust, slow and steady, into my mouth.

God, his moans sound downright sinful.

When he pulls out, I pout, but he covers my hand with his, stroking until he comes. I lean into it, letting the warmth coat my chest.

Claude leans forward and kisses me, drawing me into his lap, careless of the mess I'm making of his clothes and his couch. He holds me against him and sighs.

A few moments pass in peaceful silence with the television still chattering in the background.

"I love you, Gwen."

"Good, 'cause I love you too," I murmur. "Can I stay here forever?"

"That's a stupid question." He kisses my forehead. "Of course you can."

"How will this work? Me being dead and all?"

Claude strokes my shoulder. "Don't worry. We've got this under control."

"We?"

"Shh." He squeezes me tight. "I'll explain later. Right now, I just want to enjoy the moment."

"Okay." I bite my lip. "Can we go back to bed now?"

His laugh rumbles through me. "You're insatiable."

"Is that a yes?"

"Yes."

He helps me to my feet and follows me into the bedroom, where he shows me just how much he loves me. Over and over again.

We're two lonely hearts who have finally found their place in a world without glitz and glamour, wrapped up in each other. It's perfect, and I wouldn't have it any other way.

CHAPTER TWENTY-FIVE
CLAUDE

After a day of uninterrupted bliss, reality sets in when my brother arrives before I've had my morning coffee, banging on the door with enough force to shake the building. Grumbling under my breath, I unlock the door and swing it open.

He hasn't shaved regularly in several months, but he looks especially rough this morning. I'm sure he caught hell from Quinn for tagging along on the raid and getting caught at the wrong end of DeLuca's rage.

"You look like hell."

"Thanks." He comes in, closing the door behind him. "Where is she?"

"Shower." I pick up my coffee mug and take a sip. "Want some?"

"Sure."

"Help yourself." I stifle a grin behind my mug when he bitches under his breath and turns to the cabinet where I keep the cups.

Grant pours some coffee into the biggest cup I own and cradles it in his massive hand before inhaling deeply. I sit at the table and motion for him to join me.

"Any problems at the station?" I ask as he settles in the chair near the wall.

"Nothing McMasters couldn't handle. It took a little paper shuffling, but I think we've come to a compromise."

"Good." Relief chases away my remaining uncertainty.

"What's going on in here?" Gwen's sweet voice interrupts us.

I pivot in my chair to drink in the sight of her wearing one of my flannel shirts and sweatpants. Her damp hair lays over her shoulder as she runs her fingers through it.

My pulse flutters at her presence. How has she consumed me so entirely in such a short period of time?

When she steps within reach, I pull her into my lap, uncaring of my brother's obvious discomfort at the display of affection. She wraps her arms around my neck and kisses me softly.

"Am I interrupting?" Her attention shifts to Grant who drops his gaze to the murky bottom of his coffee cup.

"Not at all," I say.

She shifts off my lap and into the chair beside me. "Good morning, detective."

"Grant." My brother finally joins the conversation. "Just call me Grant."

"Okay." She takes my coffee mug and sips the rich dark brew.

Grant reaches into his jacket pocket and pulls out a folded piece of paper. Gwen blinks when he offers it to her. She carefully unfolds it and reads the contents. Her full lips purse and her brow furrows in confusion as she skims the words.

"Is this…?" Her voice fades.

"Your official death certificate." Grant leans back in his chair with a smile. "As of today, you're no longer Gwendolyn Monroe."

She presses a hand to her throat. "Who am I?"

"Whoever you want to be."

My brother and I share a look.

He clears his throat and continues. "You'll need a new name, new look, new paperwork, the works. Just give me the details, and I'll have the documents made as soon as possible."

"How?" she asks.

"I know some people." Grant smirks.

"Is this legal?" Gwen bites her lip. Her luminous gaze shifts between us. She's worried, but there's relief in her eyes.

"Does it matter?"

I turn to stare at Grant. My brother—the rule follower and ace detective—stepping outside the confines of the law twice in one year. Will the surprises never cease?

"No, I guess it doesn't." Gwen's shoulders soften. "How did you manage to pull this off?"

"It was easier to get you away from your family if your fiancé murdered you before he killed himself. Saves you from a long, drawn-out trial." A sincere smile lights his face, and I'm reminded of my brother's soft side. "It all worked out."

"Thank you." Tears fill her eyes. "How can I ever repay this kindness?"

"Promise me one thing." Grant stands and shoves his hands in his pockets.

"Anything."

"Take good care of my brother." He winks at her, and I shake my head. "But seriously, use this opportunity to start fresh. You've got your freedom now. Embrace it."

"I will." Gwen rests her hand on my shoulder. "Thank you so much. For everything."

Grant gives us both a resolute nod before leaving the apartment. I follow Gwen to the door and wrap my arm around her waist after she slides the lock into place. She leans back against me and sighs in contentment.

"You're a free woman now," I whisper in her ear. "What do you want to do first?"

She turns around and rests her hand against my chest.

A million stray thoughts flash through my mind, but one lingers, strong and insistent, pulsing in my brain. I hold onto it, biting my tongue until she speaks.

"Seduce you."

I laugh, and the sound echoes around the room. My mood lightens at her mischievous smile. "I mean *aside* from that."

She slides her arms around me, embracing me tightly. I rest in her hug and hold my breath.

"I don't know."

"Have you thought about who you want to be now?"

She skews up her nose, as though pondering the possibilities. I want to kiss along the bridge of her nose and bury my face in her hair.

"What about a new name?" I ask, unable to bear the

torment of impatience.

"Can I keep Gwen? Most people knew me by Gigi."

"We can ask Grant, but if we make a few other changes—dye your hair, change your wardrobe—I don't think anyone would notice your passing resemblance to a wealthy socialite's deceased daughter."

"You make it sound so illicit and suspicious."

"It is." I chuckle when she frowns at me. "What about a surname?"

"Richards has a nice ring to it." She stills against me and meets my gaze.

My heart pounds, and my breath catches in my chest. "You want to take my last name?"

"Can I?" She licks her lips.

"That's awfully presumptuous of you. Staying with me. Sharing my bed. Borrowing my name." The comment is made in jest, but it burrows beneath her skin.

"If you don't want me to, then I can pick something else." She steps back, and I regret my teasing comment. "I'll go if it's too much—"

I grab her wrist and pull her back. She tilts her chin up, tears in her eyes.

I'm making a mess of this, but I've lived alone for so long, I don't know how to share my life with anyone. How to care for anyone but myself. The one thing I've always wanted is finally within my grasp, and I'm floundering.

"Gwen." I manage to find the words, even though they terrify me with their implication. "I love you."

"But?" She sighs and tightens her grip on my flannel shirt.

"I want more." Losing myself in her eyes, it pours free. "I want you to marry me. The thought of living another moment without you in my life fucking terrifies me. Take my name as yours. Share your life with me. I promise I'll care for you until my final breath."

With a gasp, her tears break free. She jumps into my arms, pulling me down to her level, and kisses me soundly on the lips.

The taste of her consumes me. With a moan, she deepens

the kiss, drawing me into her. When I finally break away, we're both panting and I'm desperate to be inside her again.

"Is that a yes?" My voice is breathless and hoarse.

"Yes." She cups my cheek in her warm palm. "I will marry you, Claude. That's what I want. To be yours. Forever."

"Then why didn't you just say that?"

"Why didn't you ask me?"

"Because I didn't think you'd want a broken man like me." I groan when she rubs against me.

"You're not broken. You're beautiful."

Gwen beams, and I swear I'm transported by her faith in me, even if I don't believe it myself.

"I think you need your eyes checked." I scoff.

She grips my jaw in her hand and forces me to look at her. "You listen to me, Claude Richards. You're the most beautiful soul I've ever met. You took me in when I had nowhere to go. You believed in me when no one else did. I love you. Do you understand?"

"I do."

"Good." She takes my hand. "Now, come with me."

"Where are we going?" I feign stupidity as she drags me to the bedroom.

"Where I should have taken you the first night we met."

"Wait." I stop outside the door and drop her hand.

"What now?" She props her hand on her hip.

"Are you telling me I slept on the sofa for no reason?"

A wicked smile curves her lips. "I wouldn't say *no* reason. You were being a gentleman, and that made me love you more."

"Mm-hmm." My mumbled grunt only makes her laugh.

"Thank you for being my knight in shining armor, Claude. It's nice to know chivalry isn't dead."

"Gwen."

"Yes."

"Stop talking and get into bed."

"With pleasure."

EPILOGUE
GWEN

I wake up at six a.m. on Christmas morning and squeal when I see the fresh dusting of snow on the rooftops and streets outside. Claude rolls over and pulls the blanket up, burying his face. No amount of cajoling will pull him from the warmth of our bed. Not even the promise of fresh coffee and chocolate chip cookies.

"Last Christmas" plays on the radio while I finish mixing the cookie dough. I take a bite before popping the first tray into the oven. The sweet fragrance fills the air in the apartment. I've never baked cookies before, so I hover near the oven in case I forget and burn the whole building down.

Singing along to holiday music, I bustle around the apartment, making sure everything is tidy before our guests arrive at noon. Claude insisted we host the celebration in the bar. More room, he claimed. I want to surprise him before the festivities start, and I don't need an audience.

"Smells good."

I whip around at the compliment. Claude's new flannel pajamas match my own, and his hair is sticking up at odd angles. He looks adorably messy, and part of me wants to drag him back to bed, cookies and Christmas be damned.

"Thanks." I pull myself together and manage to remove the last tray of cookies from the oven without incident. After I set them on the stovetop to cool, he wraps his arm around me.

His scent mingles with the sweet aroma of chocolate chip cookies. I close my eyes and lean into him. There's nothing outside of him, outside of us.

"Merry Christmas, wife." The deep rumble of his voice against my neck unleashes a flurry of butterflies in the pit of my stomach.

Only two days have passed since we stood before a minister to recite our vows, and I still get chills when Claude calls me *wife*. The title fills me with pride and desire. After years of being trapped in my parents' shadows, I'm no longer beholden to their demands. The woman I was is gone. Dead and buried. A new, stronger version of myself stands tall beside this man, who selflessly came to the aid of a stranger. A man I chose. I wouldn't be where I am without him. And although the journey was rough, I wouldn't trade it for anything. Claude has given me the future I always dreamed of. The freedom I've always longed for. I can never repay him for his kindness, but I can show him exactly how much it means to me.

"I got you a present." He goes still at my statement.

"A present? You didn't have to do that."

"I wanted to." I take his hand. "Come here."

He trudges behind me as I pull him to the couch. When he sits, I kneel beside the tree and reach as far back as I can until my fingers find a box tucked out of sight.

"What is it?" He eyes me suspiciously.

"Open it and find out." I hand him the brightly wrapped box. Anticipation pulses through me, and I bounce on my toes.

He pats the couch beside him, and I curl up in the spot. He slowly unwraps the gift, using his knees to hold it steady as he tears the paper. His brow rises at the sight of a plain box beneath the wrapping.

A grin spreads across my lips. I try to hide it behind my hands, but he chuckles and shakes his head at my excitement.

Claude sets the box in his lap and lifts the lid, his grip encompassing it with ease. Shifting the paper aside, he laughs.

"Stephen King." He pulls a pristine, first-print copy of *The Dark Tower* from the box.

"I know you already have a copy. But this one is special." I gesture to the cover. "Look inside."

He flips the first few pages. There, on the title page, is a note scrawled in blue ink with the author's signature.

"To Claude. Enjoy, Steve King," he reads aloud in a somber tone.

"Do you like it?" I bite my lip.

"I love it." He sets the book aside and pulls me into his lap. The brush of his lips against mine drives away any reservations. When it ends, he leans his forehead against mine. "How in the world did you get this?"

"I called in a favor."

"Marcy." Claude sighs when I nod. "How did you know this was my favorite book?"

"Quinn told me."

"Thank you." He cups my cheek in his hand. "I don't have your gift here."

My brow furrows. "What gift? I thought we weren't doing gifts."

"So did I."

My face warms at his pointed look. "Point taken." I clear my throat and redirect the conversation. "Maybe we should get ready for the party? I still have some things to set up downstairs."

"Can't we just call it off and go back to bed?" He squeezes my hip, and it takes all my effort not to succumb to those seductive brown eyes luring me in.

"No. It's too late to cancel now." I scramble off his lap before he kisses me again. "Let's go."

With a grumble, Claude retreats to the shower while I clean up the kitchen and put the cookies into a Tupperware container. I manage to trade places with him without being pulled into bed, and an hour later, we descend to the bar.

Quinn and Grant arrive shortly after us and help finalize the decorations. Rob and Marcy knock on the door promptly at noon. But at twelve-thirty, there's still no sign of Arthur and Kate.

"I wonder where they are," Rob says, glancing at his watch. "It's not like Arthur to be late."

By one, Rob's pacing the floor. "I'm calling him."

I place the phone on the bar in front of him beside the Crock-Pots keeping our Christmas meal warm.

The door bursts open with a gust of wind, reminding me of the first night I entered the Black Penny. Kate and Arthur step through, shaking off the cold.

"We were about to call in a missing person's report," Grant says as he closes the door behind them.

"You might have to." Arthur turns to him with a somber look.

"What's wrong?" I straighten up at the worry etching his handsome face.

"Cyril didn't show up this morning." He runs his fingers through his hair. "He was supposed to pick us up at ten thirty. I waited until eleven and tried to call him, but there was no answer. No one has seen him since late last night."

"Maybe he had a late night out?" I offer, hopeful.

"No, he drove us home last night and told us he was stopping to pick up the purse Kate left at the party." Arthur shakes his head. "This isn't like him. I've known him for years. He's worked for me for ten. He's never been late, let alone not shown up. Something's wrong."

Kate rests a hand on her husband's arm. "It'll be okay. We'll find him."

"I'll make some calls," Grant offers.

"Thanks." Arthur sighs. "I'm sorry. I didn't mean to ruin Christmas."

"You didn't ruin anything," I assure him. "I'm sure we'll hear something soon. Let's eat, keep our strength up."

Cyril's disappearance hangs heavy over the gathering, but we manage to grasp a few joyful moments.

"I'd like to propose a toast." Rob stands and holds his glass aloft. "To 1985, a year none of us will ever forget."

"To 1985," we all echo and drink.

"To finding our soulmates," Kate adds with a bashful smile.

I catch Claude staring at me as I drink to Kate's toast. He winks, and I warm from the end of my nose to the tips of my toes. If there's one thing this year has taught me, it's to expect the unexpected and make the most of every day.

Surrounded by my new family and friends, I'm finally where I'm meant to be.

Home.

"Come with me," Claude whispers in my ear and takes me by the hand.

I lace my fingers through his and follow him down the hall to his office.

"What are you up to?" I ask when he closes the door behind us.

He pins me against the door and kisses me. All my questions disappear into smoke and drift away. I run my fingers through his hair and deepen the kiss. God, I love this man.

With a curse, he takes a step back. "I wanted to…give you this." He reaches into his pocket and pulls out a small leather box.

My eyes fly wide, and my heart flutters.

"It's my grandmother's." He opens the lid and I gasp.

A round sapphire nestled on a simple gold band winks up at me. "Claude, it's lovely."

"Do you like it?"

"I love it." With reverence, I take the ring from the velvet and slip it on my finger. It fits perfectly. Tears fill my eyes.

"I would have given it to you sooner, but I had to get it resized and—"

"Claude." I place a finger over his lips. "Stop talking and kiss me."

Without hesitation, he does just that.

"Merry Christmas, wife."

"Merry Christmas, husband." I grin. "I love you."

He beams down at me. "I know."

Before I can say anything more, he kisses me again. All thoughts of our guests and Christmas dinner are forgotten.

There's only him and me.

And that's all I'll ever need.

THE END

OTHER BOOKS BY KIRSTEN S. BLACKETER

CRAVING 1985 SERIES
When I Found You
Can't Fight This Feeling
She Gives Love a Bad Name
Owner of a Lonely Heart
Just What I Needed

HISTORICAL
An Irresistible Shadow
A Shadow's Kiss
Mississippi Moonshine
Deceiving the Earl
Jewel of Winter
At Winter's Demand
Under Winter's Control
Seducing Winter's Gentleman
Stealing the Widow's Heart
Seduction on the Alpine Express
Temptation on the Alpine Express

CONTEMPORARY
A Lockdown Love Affair
A Holiday Love Affair
Mistletoe and Mistakes
Confessions of a Fangirl
Confessions of a Gamer Girl
Confessions of a Glamour Girl
The Flight Before Christmas

FANTASY/FAIRY TALE
Curse of the Huntsman's Jewel
The Huntsman's Revenge

PIRATES AND PERSUASION
Queen Takes Hook

ABOUT THE AUTHOR

Kirsten S. Blacketer is a multi-published indie author of both historical and contemporary romance. When she's not writing, she homeschools her two children and enjoys time with her family. In those moments of freedom, she devours romance novels while sipping a glass of wine. Age has only shown her that writing villains can be just as fun as heroes. Her next life goals are to write a New York Times Bestseller and one day have Adam Driver play a starring role in a film version of one of her books. A girl can dream, right?

Read more at **http://kirstensblacketer.com.**

ALSO WRITES AS JEN BRADLEE